Plays That'll Preach

PLAYS THAT'LL PREACH

ROBERT DON HUGHES

BROADMAN PRESS
Nashville, Tennessee

4268-12
ISBN: 0-8054-6812-9

Dewey Decimal Classification: 812
Subject Headings: BIBLE – HISTORY OF BIBLICAL EVENTS – DRAMA
Library of Congress Catalog Card Number: 85-365
Printed in the United States of America

Library of Congress Cataloging in Publication Data

Hughes, Robert Don, 1949-
  Plays that'll preach.

  1. Bible plays. I. Title.
PS3558.U389P55 1985   813'.54   85-365
ISBN 0-8054-6812-9

Contents

Introduction   7

Suggestions for Production   9

1. Out of Darkness . . . (Acts 9:1-18)   11
2. Wrestling (Gen. 32:24-30)   35
3. God Appointed a Worm (Jonah 4:7-11)   55
4. An Eclipse of the Son (Mark 23:34-45)   75
5. A Door of Faith (Acts 15:27)   89
6. The Rainbow on Its Edge (Gen. 9:8-17)   115
7. Sculpture in River Mud (Gen. 4:1-8,25-26)   139
8. With Bonds of Love (Hos. 11:4-9)   165

Introduction

I'm a preacher. There are few things I love to do more, as my seminary students would probably tell you; I occasionally turn my teacher's lecturn into a pulpit! We preachers have a problem today, however: It's just so hard to compete with television! And, if the truth be known, while I love to preach I probably enjoy a good Christian film or play more than I do a sermon. Why? Because it *lives.* The characters breathe, think, act—and in their actions, the hand of God is revealed.

The Bible is filled with stories of people who encounter God through history. Most important, it contains the story of the *one* who gives history meaning. The preacher's hardest question arises again, day after day: "How can I get this most critical message across to the people who really need it?"

The answer is, we can't. Not unless they are listening. In this day and age, how do we get people to listen? We all say it all the time: "Actions speak louder than words." We must act it out before them!

Is the world listening to anything these days? Oh yes! Much more than ever before. Films, television—these consume more and more of our moments, not only in this country but around the world. It troubles me to think that while in the age of print the Bible was the most widely distributed message, in this modern age of media the most listened-to voices are those of currently popular secular movie producers and novelists. How do we reach the world? How do we preach to those who won't listen any longer to sermons?

Drama has been a tool for communicating spiritual truth since the world began. Simple storytelling is dramatic. The ritual activities of the Jewish priesthood were dramatic. Talk

7

about dramatic, look at the strange antics of the prophet Ezekiel! And never in the history of this world has there been any more dramatic act than the crucifixion, burial, and resurrection of Jesus Christ.

When I was a boy, God spoke to me through drama. As a preacher's kid growing up in Southern California I had learned early how to filter out my father's words. But on those occasions when Christian drama was performed in our church, my spirit came alive. One night when my parents were out visiting prospects I sat at home watching *Green Pastures* on television—and wept with a new understanding of the Father's sacrificial love.

Ever since, I've been preaching through drama. Now, there are a lot of reasons for doing plays—they're entertaining, certainly, and they can be educational. But the plays collected here are sermons: sermons in dramatic form. As a pastor and as a missionary I've preached the general ideas of each of these from the pulpit. But I'm convinced that for *maximum* impact, the stories ought to be played before an audience.

That's hard work. Acting and directing are skills that must be developed through experience. But I'm convinced that anyone can learn these skills if the motivation is high enough and if the material warrants that much effort. If you want to see the gospel proclaimed, the motivation ought to be there in you. I hope these plays will provide worthy material.

Suggestions for Production

Directors of Christian plays, whether in churches, on the mission field, or in Christian institutions, tend to have the same basic problems:

(1) There are too few trained, dedicated actors to fill all the roles needed.

(2) All the memorization, blocking, and polish rehearsals that go into a play are not worth the effort for just a single, solitary performance.

(3) Plays that are performed in churches must have a certain "feel" to be considered worthy material for a worship service—they also have to be the right *length* (more than twenty minutes, less than forty-five minutes) in order to "substitute" for the sermon.

(4) Most churches don't want their sanctuary cluttered up with elaborate, realistic sets . . . at least, not for any longer than the *one* performance.

What's the director to do? If the pastor would *like* to use dramatic materials like the plays in this collection, how does he go about it?

After years of experience and observation, I make these suggestions:

(1) Find a director who is highly motivated to use drama to communicate the gospel. She or he may have a lot of experience or may not—the most important thing is the *desire.* I view it as a calling to a special ministry.

(2) Let that person organize a small troupe of talented young adults. These could be professionally or college trained, or have no experience at all—once again, the desire to share the message in this way is the critical

9

element. You may be surprised (I often am!) at how
many people in our churches *do* feel just this sense of
calling. Sadly, in many churches their call is ignored
because the leadership doesn't know anything about
drama or is afraid no one would be interested.

(3) Let that group perform some of the dramatic sermons
included here in place of the traditional sermon.
There are other good plays available as well—read
some; see if they will preach; and if so, *perform* them.

(4) Encourage that troupe to share its dramatic ministry
with other churches. Doing a particular play three,
four, or a dozen times really adds to the actor's understanding both of the message of the play and of the
nature of the dramatic ministry.

(5) Try to get the troupe onto the local cable channel to
perform the play for an audience that will *never* enter
your church. Most cable companies are required to
provide "local access" time to groups just like this
troupe. For permission for local cable production of
these plays, write to Legal Consultant, Sunday School
Board of the Southern Baptist Convention, 127 Ninth
Avenue, North, Nashville, Tennessee 37234.

These plays were all written for small casts: It's less hassle to
get a small group together often for needed rehearsals. They
were written for bare stages, for the most part: All you need to
do is move the pulpit. They were written to be toured: A small
cast can travel easily to other churches and do the play there,
especially if the only set change needed is to move the pulpit.

Most of all, they were written to be *done*—to be performed.
While it may read well, a play comes to life only when it's "put
on its feet." These plays will preach. Will you give them a
chance?

Out of Darkness . . .

A One-Act Play on the Call of Paul

This play was written originally to be performed as the theme interpretation of the 1985 Baptist World Congress in Los Angeles. Like many of the other plays in this collection, its strength is in the humanness of its characters. Paul—or rather Saul, here —is a real man, experiencing real personal blindness, as well as enormous internal spiritual struggles. Elizabeth is a real woman who has much in common with her sisters of today—she is strong yet sensitive, outspoken yet caring. Dele was based on some dear African friends from my missionary experience. He, too, is real, representing so many of our brothers and sisters from so many nations of the world who are sharing the gospel with their own people. But the key to it all is that Paul does not as yet realize what he is to become. He has seen the light—he has met the Lord. Still, he is only a "failed Pharisee"—and what can one man do? What indeed! What could *we* do, if we but let God use us?

Let the characters tell their tale:

Cast of Characters

Paul—a blind former Pharisee

Yusef—Paul's confused companion

Elizabeth—a strong woman—and a Christian

Dele—an African trader

11

Isaac—a leader of the Pharisees in Damascus

Ananias—God's messenger to Saul

Setting

Damascus—the home of Elizabeth, on the street called Straight

(*On the platform there is a small rough-hewn table. It is angled slightly right of center, with three benches set around it. There are sleeping mats rolled up left. There is a stairway stage right down off the platform. The platform is* ELIZABETH *'s house—the floor below it is the "street."*)

(*Light fade to black. Suddenly a brilliant light flashes on* behind *the stage, aimed into the eyes of the audience and blinding them.*)

PAUL'S VOICE: Light! So bright it hurts! Searching you out, isolating you, dazzling you with its brilliance! Light out of darkness can't help but shock you, and may even leave you blind . . . I, Saul of Tarsus, was blinded by such a light. (*Stop tape.*)

(PAUL *shuffles blindly forward, toward platform, led by* YUSEF.)

YUSEF (*extremely anxious*):   Hello? Judas! Is anyone there!

(ELIZABETH *enters UC with candle, sets it on table as she walks quickly but not hurriedly DR.*)

ELIZABETH (*gruffly*):   What is it! What's going on!

YUSEF: Where's Judas?

ELIZABETH: Wherever he can make a shekel, no doubt. The man's a merchant, I can't keep track of him. . . .

YUSEF: Let us in!

ELIZABETH: Let you in! It's the middle of the night!

YUSEF (*protesting*): The sun just went down. . . .

ELIZABETH: When I'm already asleep then that's the middle of the night!

YUSEF: Are you the wife of Judas of Damascus?

ELIZABETH: Would I be living in his house if I weren't?

YUSEF: Let us in, madame, please! I have a wounded man with me who has directed me to this house!

ELIZABETH: Who?

YUSEF: Saul of Tarsus!

ELIZABETH (*beat*): Never heard of him.

YUSEF: You . . . (*to Saul*) she says she's never heard of you!

PAUL: I'm blind, Yusef, but there's nothing wrong with my hearing. Please don't shout in my ear.

YUSEF (*impatiently*): Sorry—

PAUL: Dear lady, I know your husband—

ELIZABETH: Now *that* I don't doubt. He knows every John, Jacob, and Joseph from here to the streets of Rome.

PAUL: My name is Paul.

ELIZABETH: He knows every Paul too. Well, don't just stand there, come on in.

(PAUL *and* YUSEF *climb steps, then* YUSEF *steps back.*)

YUSEF: I'll . . . visit you later, Paul. (*He turns to go.*)

ELIZABETH: Here now, wait just a moment!

YUSEF: I have important business with the leaders of your synagogue! (*He exits.*)

ELIZABETH: You can't mean you're just going to dump him here on . . . me . . .? (*To self.*) That's exactly what he means! But then, why not? I *am*, after all, nothing but a Jewish wife. (*To* PAUL.) All right, bosom friend of my wandering spouse, you can sit over there.

PAUL: Where?

ELIZABETH: Right there! (*Pointing.*)

PAUL (*bitterly*): I can't see.

ELIZABETH: Oh, now *that's* good news! (*She takes his hand to lead him.*)

PAUL: I hear your frustration, Elizabeth—and you're *going* to hear a lot more about it! I'm getting some insight, I think, into why Judas spends so much time traveling.

ELIZABETH (*harshly*): Sit down! (PAUL *sits above table.* ELIZABETH *sits left of it. Beat.*) Now. Suppose you explain what's going on?

PAUL (*humorless chuckle*): Ah! Dear lady. *No one* would like to know that more than I!

ELIZABETH (*sarcastic*): Now, I'm not so sure of that. I'm

rather curious about all this myself. (*Harshly.*) What's going on!

PAUL: A group of us were bound here to Damascus from Jerusalem on—Temple business.

ELIZABETH: Well, I gathered it had something to do with the priests by what your friend said as he bolted out of here.

PAUL: I must apologize for Yusef. He's had a difficult day.

ELIZABETH: *He* has!

PAUL: As have I, and, I suppose, as you have.

ELIZABETH: I know *my* problems. What's the matter with Yusef?

PAUL: He believes that I've gone mad.

(ELIZABETH *starts slowly and steps away.*)

ELIZABETH: Well, now. That would explain the strangeness of your sudden appearance at my door, but I can hardly say it makes me *feel* any better.

PAUL: Dear lady, I am not mad.

ELIZABETH: I'm not all that dear, Saul, as perhaps you've noticed. Call me Elizabeth. And tell me why your friend thinks you *are?*

PAUL (*sighs*): About midday, we were within—

ELIZABETH: Who's we?

PAUL: Ah—a party of the Pharisees.

ELIZABETH: You're a Pharisee?

PAUL: Of course I'm a Pharisee!

ELIZABETH: Figures. Are you hungry? I have some dates.

PAUL (*sighs hungrily*):   No.

ELIZABETH: Well, *I'm* hungry. (*She rises, goes upstage to pick up pottery bowl of dates.*) Go on with your tale.

PAUL: A party of us were on our way to Damascus when—

ELIZABETH: These are very good. . . .

PAUL: Madame, do you wish to hear or not?

ELIZABETH: I said I did, so what happened at noon today?

PAUL (*Beat. Then with less formality*):   My life was forever altered.

ELIZABETH (*widens eyes meaningfully*):   Go on.

PAUL: This was not the sun, madame. The sun was there, but this light was far brighter than the sun's golden radiance, and it was directly in front of us too, as if hovering protectively over Damascus, over those we'd come to harm.

ELIZABETH: Harm? Who were you coming to harm?

PAUL (*evasively*):   It was—a searching light, a piercing light, penetrating not only the eyes but the spirit as well. And I, on my knees, could do nothing but stare into it! (*Pause.*) And then, after an eternal instant, a voice spoke to me: "Saul!" it said—it called me by name, it knew my name! "Saul!" it said again, "Why are you persecuting me?" (*Pause.*)

ELIZABETH (*with mystery*):   Did . . . Yusef hear this voice?

PAUL: Yes! But he didn't understand it.

ELIZABETH: Ah. But he did see the light?

PAUL: Yes! No . . . (*Thinking.*) No. Esais saw the light, but not Yusef.

ELIZABETH: Oh. And did Esais understand the voice?

PAUL: He didn't hear it. Madame—Elizabeth—Elizabeth, I know it must sound ridiculous to you; but I tell you, these things *happened,* and they've changed my life forever! Look at my eyes! (*He leans toward her.*) You see?

ELIZABETH: I see . . . eyes, but . . .

PAUL: They're open, then?

ELIZABETH: Certainly they're open.

PAUL: Yet I see *nothing.* A black pit. Nothing at all. (*He sits back in his seat.*)

ELIZABETH: Well. It's evident you're very agitated—

PAUL: Would you not be?

ELIZABETH: And evident, too, why Yusef was so anxious to be rid of you.

PAUL: No, no, Elizabeth, it wasn't that experience that made them think me mad. They didn't see what *I* saw, or hear what I heard; but they did see and hear *something,* and it terrified them. But what frightened them most was the *change* they saw in me, a sudden, inexplicable reversal. I had led them here to attack an enemy, and suddenly I was *talking* to that enemy on the road.

ELIZABETH: What enemy? Who was this . . . light that
    spoke?

PAUL: He called himself Jesus.

ELIZABETH (*doubtfully, rising slowly*):   Jesus?

PAUL: There are many called Jesus, I know. This is an obscure
    Nazarene who was recently executed for fomenting rebel-
    lion.

ELIZABETH (*holding her hands, stepping away*):   Jesus
    . . .

PAUL (*thoughtfully*):   Although I have cause, now, to doubt
    that charge. . . .

ELIZABETH: And you came here to persecute his followers?

PAUL: Yes . . . The ones who call themselves the followers of
    the Way.

ELIZABETH (*after a pause*):   Why here? Why did you come
    to *this* house?

PAUL: When . . . (*quietly*) When the light had gone away, and
    I began to speak of my vision, my brother Pharisees wanted
    nothing to do with me. They fled, in fact, leaving me on the
    road, obviously blind and, I'm sure, seeming half out of my
    mind. Only Yusef took pity on me and came back to guide
    me into the city, inquiring all the way for some place he
    might leave me. I knew no one in Damascus except other
    Pharisees, but I remembered one Judas who lived some-
    where here on the street named Straight. I sold him some
    tents once.

ELIZABETH (*a bit relieved*):   Oh yes, he wears tents out
    quickly. Certainly he never spends anytime *here*. . . .

PAUL: We began to ask directions, and everyone we spoke to—

ELIZABETH: . . . Knew Judas of Straight Street. Of course. (ELIZABETH *sighs, puts her hands on her hips, and looks around.*) Now then. What am I to do with you?

PAUL: The heavenly vision told me to come here and wait, that someone would come to—But to you that must sound like still further madness.

ELIZABETH: No, friend Paul. I don't believe you're at *all* mad. (PAUL *shifts position, letting down somehow, as if feeling welcome at last.*) You're exhausted. I'll fetch you a sleeping mat. (*She goes UC, brings sleeping mat, and spreads it downstage of table. Then she steps back to take his hand.*)

PAUL: I know this is highly unusual, Elizabeth, for a woman in the absence of her husband to give lodging to a man—

ELIZABETH: The people of Damascus have come to expect the unusual of Elizabeth. And should anyone question me, I'll just say you're a part of my family. You are, of course.

PAUL: I . . . ?

ELIZABETH: Lay down. Rest. (*He does.*) There'll be more time to talk. Oh, let me blow out the light.

PAUL: As you please. *I've* been plunged forever into blindness.

ELIZABETH: As to that, brother Paul . . . we shall see. (*She blows out light.*)
(*Cue tape.*)

PAUL'S VOICE: At midday, oh king, I saw in the way a light from heaven, above the brightness of the sun, shining round about myself and those with me. And when we'd all fallen to the ground, I heard a voice in the Hebrew tongue.

VOICE: Saul, Saul, why do you persecute me?

PAUL'S VOICE: And I said, "Who are you, Lord?"

VOICE: I am Jesus, the one you are persecuting. Stand upon your feet, for I have appeared to you to make you a witness —both of what you've already seen, and other things I will show you. I'm sending you not just to your own people, but to the whole world—to open the eyes of the unbelievers— to turn them from darkness to light . . .
Darkness to light . . . Darkness to light . . .
Darkness to light . . .

CLAP! CLAP! (*An African trader stands at steps clapping his hands.*)

DELE: Halloo? Halloo? It is morning, is there someone to greet me? (PAUL *bolts up on his mat*—ELIZABETH *enters UC and hurries to the door.*)

ELIZABETH (*snappishly*):   Who's there?

DELE: I am a traveler, a trader. Is this the dwelling of Judas the merchant?

ELIZABETH: Rarely. You know my husband?

DELE (*going upstairs*):   Madame, in my land *everyone* knows your husband.

ELIZABETH: Why am I not surprised? Come in, come in. (PAUL *has gotten to his feet and found his way to the table to sit left of it.*) This is Paul, born of Tarsus—but you may not know where that is. . . .

DELE: I've been there many times.

ELIZABETH: Oh. And Paul, this is. . . . What is your name?

DELE: I think you would not be able to say it all, so why put your tongue to the test? Call me Dele.

ELIZABETH: Please, sit. I'll bring food. (*She runs UC.*)

PAUL: Where are you from, Dele?

DELE: The south.

PAUL: Ah. The deserts?

DELE: Further south.

PAUL: Egypt?

DELE: Still further. I am from the land your people call Ethiopia, but we don't call it that at all. (*Taking food.*) Thank you, Madame.

PAUL: And you are a trader. What do you trade?

DELE: Everything. It's too far to travel not to take a bit of everything in the journey.

ELIZABETH: I'm sorry to disappoint you, but my husband isn't here.

DELE: Of course not, for I left him in Alexandria. He sends you his greetings and apologizes that he didn't have time to write.

ELIZABETH (*wide-eyed, nods and shrugs*): But . . . is that why you're here? Just to bring his greetings?

DELE: It's an important reason, is it not? But that's not all. I've come here by way of Samaria, and there are wonderful things happening there that have made me curious. I inquired in the market and have learned that you might have information for me about God.

PAUL: About . . . God? Are you speaking to me?

DELE: With all respect, sir—I addressed the lady.

PAUL: But she's—

ELIZABETH: Brother Paul, I said there would be a time to talk further. When you said last night you'd come to persecute the followers of the Way, my heart leaped so high I thought it would choke me. *I* am a follower of the Way.

PAUL (*surprised*):   Then—you knew about this Jesus. . . .

ELIZABETH: I prefer to say *I know Jesus.* He lives.

PAUL (*after a moment*):   Yes—he does.

DELE (*a bit impatiently*):   So then, my friends, tell *me* about this Jesus!

PAUL: You want to know?

DELE: Should I not?

PAUL: But if you're from Ethiopia—

DELE (*sadly*):   Ah ah. I know what I shall hear. You are a *Gentile;* you have your own gods. You see, I have been to your Temple, and they would not let me inside. I do not understand you people! You say "God is one," and my people know that as well as yours, yet you will not let your God be God to us as well.

ELIZABETH: Perhaps if we talked of other thi—

DELE: Wait! My friend of Tarsus. If God has done something wonderful in Jerusalem, He has done it for the *whole world*. It's good news! So why do you sit upon it, as the elders do when they hide scandals? (PAUL *sits speechless, his face turned away from Dele's, lost in thought.*) It doesn't matter. If someone will tell me exactly what God has done, I will go back to my people and *I* will tell them. It's best that way. They'll believe *me*.

ELIZABETH: Listen—Dele, is it?

DELE: Yes, Madame.

ELIZABETH: There is a man who can explain the way far better than I . . . if you'll step outside with me I'll point out the way to his house.

DELE: I'm grateful. (*They step to the stairway and down;* ELIZABETH *points and mimes directions as* PAUL *quotes Scripture to himself.*)

PAUL: "Thus says the Lord, I have called you in righteousness, I will also hold you by the hand and watch over you, and I will appoint you as a covenant to the people, . . . as a light to the nations . . . to open blind eyes. . . ." (*Rising, turning to step toward center.*) "The people who walk in darkness will see a great light; Those who live in a dark land, The light will shine on them." Blind. (ELIZABETH *is back into the room.*) Blindness.

ELIZABETH: What?

PAUL: I've been so blind! The Scriptures are clear; the *need* is clear! *This* is the mystery, the plan of the ages, hidden in Jesus Christ and only *now* revealed in Him! God wants to change the whole world!

(*From UR and UL enter flag bearers.*)

PAUL: Elizabeth, I see. . . .

ELIZABETH: You *see?* Your sight's returned?

PAUL: No . . . not that sight. And yet I see . . . The emblems
of many nations, furled upon the breeze, the colors of peoples and lands. They swirl through my mind, proud symbols, all . . . the same in this: Jesus Christ will be known and
loved in each. Look! Green and white; black, red, and gold;
red, white, and blue; a red sun on a field of purest white—
Elizabeth. Jesus Christ will be preached and praised in
each of these.

ELIZABETH (*has stepped to his side—worriedly*): Paul, are
you all right?

PAUL: I am . . . overwhelmed. To see the world . . . and know
that it is one in Christ Jesus . . . (*He watches as the last flag
swirls past, then allows himself to be led back to his chair,
left of the table.*)

ELIZABETH: Are you hungry? You haven't eaten.

PAUL: I'm fine, Elizabeth.

ELIZABETH: Can I get you anything?

PAUL: Perhaps . . . perhaps you could find a corner for me to
sit in and think?

ELIZABETH (*nods, a bit sadly*): Over here. (*She leads him
DL, sits him on a mat, then crosses back to DR stairs.*) (*To
herself.*) I wonder when he'll come. . . .

(*Lights fade to black. PAUL moves down left to sleeping mat;
ELIZABETH is off UC again. Lights up. ISAAC enters, angry,
his robes billowing, followed by an uncertain YUSEF. ISAAC
comes to the door and shouts.*)

ISAAC: Open up! Open up in there!

ELIZABETH (*reenters bearing candle, rubbing her eyes, grumpily*): Judas, if this is somebody else wanting to buy your trinkets I'm going to boil you in your own olive oil.

ISAAC: Would you open this door!

ELIZABETH (*angry*): What is it with you people! I haven't had a decent night's sleep in three days! (*She goes to stairs, calls down.*) Judas isn't here!

ISAAC (*frowning*): Who?

ELIZABETH: My wandering husband!

ISAAC (*harshly*): I know nothing about any Judas. I am Isaac, of the synagogue, and I'm come to see Saul of Tarsus! Will you admit me?

(ELIZABETH *looks over at* PAUL, *who has sat up on his mat and now clasps his arms about his knees. He's obviously tense.*)

ELIZABETH: You know someone named Isaac?

PAUL: I know *of* him.

ELIZABETH: And?

PAUL: He's the man I was coming to see.

ELIZABETH: Shall I let him in?

PAUL: It is your house, Elizabeth. (*She turns back to "door," beckons* ISAAC *to enter.* ISAAC *sweeps upstairs, followed by* YUSEF, *who avoids Elizabeth's eyes as she speaks.*)

ELIZABETH: Oh, so you decided to come back and fetch him after all?

ISAAC (*moving directly to Paul*): Are you Paul?

PAUL: I am.

ISAAC: Stand up. You're coming with us.

PAUL (*beat*):   Am I?

ISAAC: I said stand up.

YUSEF (*explaining*):   Paul, he's from the synagogue, and he
     wants to—

ISAAC (*cutting* YUSEF *off*):   I'll deal with this. Get up, Paul.

PAUL: I do not choose to get up, Isaac of Damascus. Perhaps
     you would like to sit down and explain what this is about?

ISAAC: You know quite well why I'm here.

PAUL: Do I?

ISAAC: The others in the synagogue are waiting.

PAUL: Elizabeth, is the sun up?

ELIZABETH: You haven't heard any roosters, have you?

PAUL: Why do you come in the night, Isaac? Why not wait for
     the morning?

ISAAC: A problem of this nature must not be allowed to fes-
     ter.

PAUL: I am a problem, now?

ISAAC: Delay us no further!

PAUL: Was I *not* a problem all day yesterday? Why didn't you
     come for me then?

YUSEF (*still trying to defuse the situation*): Paul, I . . . I told them of your vision—

PAUL: Then why do they need to hear it from me?

ISAAC: It is not your so-called "vision" that concerns us!

PAUL (*puzzled*): No? Then what?

ISAAC: We are troubled by your contacts with the local followers of the Nazarene! (ISAAC *turns to glare at* ELIZABETH, *who cannot help but back a step away.*) (*Pause.*)

PAUL: What are you talking about?

ISAAC (*beat, then with sarcasm*): This is Saul of Tarsus, the great enforcer of the faith in Jerusalem? Excuse me, Yusef, but I expected someone with a bit more wit!

YUSEF: He's had a difficult—

ISAAC: Silence! (YUSEF *shuts up.*) (*Back to* PAUL.) What am I talking about, you ask. (*Circling* PAUL.) I'm talking about your mission, Paul—or have you forgotten why you came to Damascus? You see, *I* now have your letters of permission from the chief priests in Jerusalem to bind and imprison any follower of "the way" you might find in this city! (*He unrolls a scroll and dangles it over* PAUL, *who of course can't see it.*) And do you now suddenly insist that you know nothing of any followers of Jesus in Damascus? I find that extremely puzzling.

PAUL (*beat*): Why?

ISAAC (*exploding*): Because it's a lie! We know you've had a change of heart, Paul, and we know you're in contact with these people! Now get up and accompany us to the synagogue, and tell us what you know! (*Grudgingly.*) Then we'll find the best doctor in Damascus to come and look at your eyes.

PAUL: A change of heart? Yes. Yes, I suppose that phrase expresses it best. As He did in David, God has created in me a clean heart—renewed my spirit. But as for contacts with these followers of the way, I know only this. . . .

(ELIZABETH'*s face freezes into a mask of restrained terror as* ISAAC *leans in to listen.*)

PAUL: They're terrified of me, and they won't come near. (ISAAC *straightens back up, frowning*—ELIZABETH *breathes.*) Would you? It appears that my reputation as a "religious warrior" has preceded me. You'd apparently heard something of it. If you were one of these followers of Jesus, would you want to have anything to do with me? (*Pause.*) Go back to your synagogue, Isaac, and tell them what you like. You've done your job. You've seen me. As for your offer of a doctor—there's only one who could heal my eyes, and he's the one who blinded me.

ISAAC: You're mad, Paul.

PAUL: So you would say.

ISAAC: It's true. Understandable, in a way. You're so obsessed with these Jesus followers, have hounded them with such abandon, that you've fallen into their fallacies and gone mad.

PAUL: Perhaps. Perhaps you're right, Isaac. But I can only hope *you* might someday have just such an obsession. (*Pause.*)

ISAAC: Yusef, it appears your friend has chosen not to help us. Come. (*He moves downstage of table to the door; there he stops and looks back to wave.*) But we'll be back. The moment I can tie you to these people, Paul, I'll be back. Remember—*I* now hold your letters! (*He exits down stairs, followed by* YUSEF.) (*Pause—*ELIZABETH *breathes.*)

ELIZABETH: They're gone.

PAUL: Good. Perhaps we can at last get some sleep.

ELIZABETH: Paul?

PAUL: Yes, Elizabeth?

ELIZABETH: Christ truly can change a person, can't he?

PAUL: He not only can—he *does.*

(*Slow fade to black.*)

(PAUL *sits again at table, looking morose.* ELIZABETH *enters up center with lighted candle.*)

ELIZABETH: Paul? The sun is gone.

PAUL: It is? I see no change.

ELIZABETH: It's been three days, Paul, and your strength is gone. You simply *must* break this fast and eat something!

PAUL: I'm not denying myself, Elizabeth; I'm simply not hungry.

ELIZABETH: Well, it's there before you, when you do. (*Pause —she moves about her business UC.*)

PAUL: Any news of the Ethiopian?

ELIZABETH: Oh, he left yesterday with a caravan of goods— and a brilliant smile. I've never seen a man so excited to get home. I wish *my* husband felt as strongly!

PAUL: You've said little about yourself through these long three days.

ELIZABETH: You seemed . . . preoccupied.

PAUL: Uuh. (*Nodding agreement.*) Visions, Elizabeth. I've seen things too marvelous for human phrases, places beyond the breadth of words.

ELIZABETH: And yet—

PAUL: Yes?

ELIZABETH: You seem so . . . unhappy.

PAUL: Unhappy? (*Thinks.*) I'm blind, dear lady. I sit in the house of a new—but already dear—friend, and wonder what I shall do. (ELIZABETH *frowns, goes to the steps, looks out.*) What about you, Elizabeth? Are *you* happy?

ELIZABETH: I don't use the word too much.

PAUL: You used it to me.

ELIZABETH: I did, didn't I?

PAUL: You strike me as being—if not *happy*—at least at peace with yourself.

ELIZABETH: Umm. (*Nodding.*) That's only recently. I used to be harsh—well, harsh*er*—angry all the time. You were right, that first day—that's why Judas won't come home. Yet I do wish he would, now that I know Jesus. I think he might be more likely to stay. I'm more patient now, and less likely to yell—

ANANIAS (*at steps*): Hello, Elizabeth? Is he still here?

ELIZABETH (*hot*): Ananias, it's about *time* you got here! Get in this house! (*She storms up center as* ANANIAS *comes up the steps.* PAUL *smiles slightly to himself.*) This poor man's been waiting three days for you to come, and—well, sit down! Paul, this is Ananias. Ananias, that's Paul.

ANANIAS: I . . . I've heard a good deal about you. . . .

ELIZABETH: Tell him the rest.

ANANIAS: In fact, I had a difficult time making myself come. You've . . . built quite a bit of notoriety for yourself, Saul, and your fearful reputation preceded you.

ELIZABETH: That's why he wouldn't come.

ANANIAS: Elizabeth, I think I can explain myself fairly well without your help.

ELIZABETH: Are you telling me to be quiet?

ANANIAS: Sh . . . yes.

ELIZABETH (*beat*): Oh.

ANANIAS (*deep breath*): Now, Saul, Elizabeth is right, of course. I should have come sooner. Then again, if I've truly heard the Lord, these days of thought and prayer have not been wasted ones for you?

PAUL: Indeed not.

ANANIAS: Then perhaps in *your* conversations with the Lord you've heard already what I've come to say. You are, you know, his chosen instrument, to proclaim his name before the whole world.

PAUL (*sighs*): The whole world? Ananias, do you have any vision of how *big* the whole world is?

ANANIAS: Not really, no. I rarely get out of Damascus.

PAUL: Elizabeth's husband could tell you, for he's traveled all over it. And it's *vast*, Ananias. It's *too* vast. Me, a vessel to carry this light to the Gentiles? How can it be done?

ANANIAS: Why . . . you'll not be alone, you know.

ELIZABETH: Is *that* what's been bothering you these past three days, causing you to grumble around here and turn up your nose at my cooking? Listen, Saul! Listen to what you yourself have said! Who knows my husband?

PAUL: Why, everybody . . .

ELIZABETH: Because he *goes!* He *does* what he does! And everybody *will* know you, because you are committed to *go!*

ANANIAS: Not quite everybody knows your husband, Elizabeth. I've never met him myself . . .

ELIZABETH: Of course not. You never leave Damascus. Pay attention, Saul. All those flags you saw in your vision. Those lands will hear of Jesus because people as excited about it as this man Dele will be eager to share their good news!

PAUL: But what does that all mean to me? (*Rising.*) Look at me, Elizabeth! What can God do with one *blind failure* of a Pharisee?

ANANIAS (*picking up the candle and putting his hand on* PAUL's *shoulder*): He can shine his light *through* you. Oh, it's just a little glimmer, I'll grant, and he's the light of the world. But you take all those little glimmers, and let them shine together, and see how quickly he can light up his world!

PAUL: I *see* that. . . .

ANANIAS: Of course.

PAUL: I can see that flame!

ANANIAS: Didn't the Lord reveal to you that I was to come
and lay hands on you, and that you were to receive your
sight?

PAUL: I can see!

ANANIAS: And that's the way the whole world will come out
of its darkness—flame by flame. Hold it up, Paul. Let it
shine.

(PAUL *takes candle, raises it above his head, turns to audience.
Music swells.*)

(Instrumental intro: "This Little Light of Mine")

VOICE ON TAPE: Let your light so shine before men, that
they may see the light of Christ in you and glorify your
Father who is in heaven. Lift up *your* light! Let it shine!

(*Music director rises to lead congregation in several choruses of
"This Little Light of Mine," and the service may then be closed
in whatever way the service leader feels is appropriate.*)

Wrestling

A One-Act Play About Jacob

This is one of my favorite sermons. In fact, it's my "sugar stick"—that sermon preachers tend to preach when called on by surprise, or when speaking before an unfamiliar group. I think it makes an even better play, however, for the *personalities* in the story of Jacob are so vivid and human that they deserve the chance to live before us.

Of all the characters in the Bible, I find Jacob one of the easiest to identify with. His (lousy) motives are so transparent! He's so obviously a cheat! If this were a soap opera, Jacob would be the focal character, the star villain who keeps trouble stirred up. This all makes Jacob's spiritual transformation more meaningful. While he meets God at Bethel ("the house of God"), he treats the Lord as just another player to be swindled. When he wrestles with God at Peniel ("the face of God"), his outlook is very different. Let the characters speak for themselves:

Cast of Characters

3 men, 3 women, 1 angel (male or female)

Jacob

Esau

Laban

Rachel

Rebecca

Leah

An Angel

Setting

Peniel, by the stream called Jabbok—Jacob is dreaming.

(*The stage is bare of any props or set pieces. The play begins in darkness. There are sounds of a scuffle and muffled groaning from* JACOB. *When the lights fade up—blues only—we see dimly a man on his knees, struggling with a standing figure in white.*)

JACOB: Please . . . please. . . .

ANGEL: You must let me go, Jacob.

JACOB: No! No, you can't go! Not until you bless me!

ANGEL: You ask for a blessing. I cannot give it until you are ready to receive it, Jacob.

JACOB: I *am* ready to receive it! I am! Oh Lord, you must! Esau waits across the river with a drawn dagger! I must be sure you are with me!

ANGEL: Hasn't the Lord been with you always, Jacob?

JACOB: Yes . . . no . . . perhaps . . . how can I tell? I don't know anything for sure anymore!

ANGEL: You're struggling.

JACOB: Yes! Struggling to . . . to remember . . . to understand myself . . . to make some sense out of this world.

ANGEL: Then remember. (*Raises his arms.*)

JACOB: What? How?

ANGEL: Your brother Esau . . . and a pot of stew. (*Blackout.*)

(*Lights up bright. JACOB is seen on his knees, down center, stirring a pantomimed pot of stew. He is humming. ESAU enters, pantomimes dropping a burden, comes slowly to* JACOB.)

ESAU (*takes deep sniff, pats stomach, smiles, but* JACOB *does not respond. ESAU clears his throat loudly.*)

JACOB (*not looking up*): Swallow a lot of dust chasing deer, older brother?

ESAU (*frowns, then forces a smile*): Is it soup yet?

JACOB: What should you care, older brother? A mighty hunter like yourself—surely you have no need for "women's soup."

ESAU (*grunts*): Listen. You know I didn't mean that.

JACOB: Do I?

ESAU: Of course you do. (*Sits.*) You're just trying to get a rise out of me because I didn't catch any game today.

JACOB: Or yesterday, or the day before that, or the day—

ESAU: Shut up! (JACOB *stops, continues to stir soup.*) Come on, Jacob, be human for once. Give your brother something to eat.

JACOB (*stands*): What's it worth to you?

ESAU(*laughs*): What have I got? Nothing you'd want.

JACOB: Maybe. Maybe not. (*Stoops to stir pot.*)

ESAU (*sniffing*): Jacob, you may not be much of a man, but you sure make a mean soup. Come on, give me a taste.

JACOB: I asked you what it was worth.

ESAU: All right. I'll play your little game. What have I got that Jacob wants? My staff? You want my staff, Jacob? No, what does a perfumed runt who sits in his mother's tent all day need with a *man's* walking stick?

JACOB (*looks up at him*): Try again.

ESAU (*thinking*): Ah . . . my knife. A good bone knife I made by hand. Is that what you want?

JACOB: I have plenty of knives.

ESAU: Ha! For cutting stew meat!

JACOB: Which none of us has tasted lately . . . because of your excellent aim, I believe.

ESAU: You want my bow, maybe? Perhaps you think you could do better? Ha! You couldn't even notch the string!

JACOB: Keep trying.

ESAU (*sits*): That's it. That's Esau's possessions in this world. So what do I have that you want?

JACOB: You really want to know?

ESAU (*exploding*): Yes, I want to know! I'm *hungry,* you *runt!*

JACOB: Very well. It's nothing of importance to you, I'm sure.

ESAU: What is it? You can have it. (*Going to soup pot.*)

JACOB: Nothing but the right of birth.

ESAU (*looks at* JACOB, *laughs*): You've been fighting for that since the day we were born, haven't you, Shorty.

JACOB: Is it any matter to you?

ESAU (*snorts*): The birthright? Ha! Can you eat it? Can you wear it? Naw! Forget it. Gimme a bowl.

JACOB: Then you give it to me?

ESAU: Take it, for what good it does you. Gimme a bowl! (JACOB *pantomimes ladling soup into a bowl, passes it to* ESAU *with a smile.*) Of course, *who* our father blesses is entirely up to him! (ESAU *chuckles, sits to pantomime eating.*)

JACOB (*folds arms across chest*): Maybe. But maybe not. (*Blackout.*)

(*Lights dim up with blues only on* JACOB *and* ANGEL, *struggling.*)

JACOB: Yes . . . yes, I remember now. But what of it?

ANGEL: Was the Lord not with you then, Jacob? Or do you think it was by sheer cunning and deceit that the right of birth passed to you instead of to your twin brother?

JACOB: I—I don't know—were you, Lord? I mean, I never thought of you being with me. Not until . . . until after the blessing. (*Blackout.*)

REBECCA (*in darkness; frightened, loud whisper*): Jacob! Jacob!

(*Blue lights up;* JACOB *lying onstage.* REBECCA *enters, kneels beside him.*)

REBECCA: Jacob, wake up!

JACOB: Wha—wha you—Mother? (*Coming awake.*)

REBECCA: Shh!

JACOB: Why are you—

REBECCA: Jacob, listen to me. Esau just left your father's tent.

JACOB (*suddenly alert*): Was he angry?

REBECCA: Angry! He threatens to kill you! He's already searching your tents. It won't be long until he realizes that I've hidden you here.

JACOB: Mother! What'll I do!?

REBECCA: Shh! I have a goatskin of water for you, food for a week's journey through the desert, and what gold I've been able to save. You must leave—

JACOB: Leave! But I've never been gone from home more than—

REBECCA: Travel as swiftly as you can to the north, my son. Stay in the hill country and cover your tracks well. Your brother is not a quick thinker but he is careful when he hunts, and with this new hatred spurring him on, you must prove more careful than he.

JACOB: But Mother! Where will I go! How long—

REBECCA: No more now! Go to Haran. My family is there. My father, if he still lives, and my brothers. Stay as long as you can—as long as God lets you.

JACOB: God?

REBECCA: Remember, my son, you bear the promise of the father Abraham! You are the chosen of God!

JACOB: You mean we tricked God, too?

REBECCA: It—it wasn't a trick. You deserved to be blessed.

JACOB: Tell Esau that.

REBECCA: You must run, or you will be telling him yourself, face to face.

JACOB (*jumps up*):   I'm going. (*Stops, looks back.*) You mean, Father's God really cares about me now? Because I tricked Esau?

REBECCA: Don't think of it as a trick, son. God was in it.

JACOB (*starts off, stops*):   Mother—I love you. (*They embrace; she pulls away, pushes his hair out of his eyes, and kisses his cheek.*)

ESAU (*offstage*):   Jacob! Jacob! Where are you!?

REBECCA (*whispering*):   Run now! (*He exits quickly; blackout.*)

(*Blues dim up on* JACOB *with* ANGEL.)

JACOB: And that night—was the first . . . that's my first memory of you! In a dream it was . . . like tonight. . . .

ANGEL: Many years ago, Jacob.

JACOB: And how many dreams since then? How many nights have you invaded my rest, leaving me in the morning with a quiet longing that's never satisfied?

ANGEL: How many times have you wrestled with your own sin, Jacob?

JACOB: Sin again. Why must you keep bringing that *word* up? I only did what anyone would do!

ANGEL: Then why do you wrestle?

JACOB: So you will bless me!

ANGEL: Then look at your sin, Jacob. Look at it!

JACOB (*lights dimming*):   Look at it? Look where?

ANGEL: There . . . (*Points downstage.*) The first visitation. The morning after you first saw the stairway to heaven and the angels descending.

JACOB: But—but that was sin?

ANGEL: Look! (*Blackout.*)

(*Lights come up bright. ANGEL is gone; JACOB is asleep. He opens his eyes, looks around, yawns, rubs his neck.*)

JACOB: Owww! That's the last time I sleep on a rock! I'll get a decent pillow if I have to pluck the duck myself. (*Stands, stretches.*) Ah. Now for some breakfast. (*Kneels, stops suddenly.*) Are you still here? God? Are you still here? I—I remember a dream—weird dream. Oh, it was just my imagination. (*Starts to get breakfast, then stops again, looking up, around, behind.*) All right, where are you? Show yourself, so we can talk! (*Silence.*) No? OK. But I can talk to you, can't I? Good. Now. Assuming you're real—assuming that my father hasn't just been putting up a big show all these years to keep Grandfather Abraham's spirit off his back—assuming you're listening to me, God—Hello? (*Pause.*) I must have cracked my head on that granite pillow last night and scrambled my brains. What am I doing?

(*Shakes his head, starts to go on about his business, stops again.*) But Mother said—(*Loudly.*) All right. Assuming you're there, ah—we'll make a deal, OK? You told me—I *think* you told me—that you would make a nation out of me. Well, that's fine. You just do that. But listen, I want to get something out of this. If you'll be with me, and keep me safe as I travel, and give me food, and—ah—clothes, I need some new clothes—and if you'll return me safely to my father's house—if you'll do all that for me, God, then I'll worship you. Well, here, I'll even set up an altar for you right here. (*Pantomimes setting up stones.*) This is a sign of our agreement, God, all right? I'll—I'll even name this place Bethel—"God's House." How's that? (*Silence.*) My father used to tell me he talks to you and you to him. Am I missing the signals, or what? (*Pause.*) Well, you think on it some anyway. If it suits you, then as far as I'm concerned we've got us a deal. All right? (*Pause.*) All right, God? (*Blackout.*)

JACOB (*in darkness*): Why would you never talk to me as you spoke to my father? Dreams, always dreams. Nothing to grab hold of, nothing—(*Blues up.*)

ANGEL: Nothing in writing, Jacob? No contract to keep hidden in the secret places of your tent?

JACOB: I—I only wanted—to be more sure, that's all. All I ever wanted to do was the right thing.

ANGEL: And didn't the Lord bless you for it?

JACOB: Yeah, you blessed me all right. I had to work my head off!

ANGEL: And wasn't it worth it?

JACOB: Worth the work? For—Rachel? (*Smiles to himself.*) Yes. *Well* worth the work, if you put it that way. (*Blackout.*)

(*Lights come up very bright and warm.* JACOB *is sitting. He is hot and keeps wiping his forehead.* RACHEL *enters behind him, puts her hands over his eyes.*)

RACHEL: Guess!

JACOB (*teasing*): Oh, well, let me see. Leah?

RACHEL (*annoyed*): Oh!! Why do you always tease me like that!

JACOB (*laughs, pulls her around in front of and into his lap*): Because, my lovely little Rachel, you are so much fun to tease!

RACHEL: You'd better watch out. One of these days my sister may just surprise you, and you'll be stuck with *her* on your lap instead of me!

JACOB: Not a chance. I'd know you from her *anywhere*.

RACHEL: How would you know?

JACOB: By the scent of your hair—the touch of your hand— the softness of your lips—(*Kisses her; she struggles to get up, fails.*)

RACHEL: Jacob! *Anyone* could be watching us!

JACOB (*laughing*): No one's watching but my sheep. Pardon me, I mean your *father's* sheep.

RACHEL: You and Daddy don't really get along, do you?

JACOB (*lets her up*): Certainly we get along. We get along fine. (*Rises.*) We're in complete agreement about one another's character. I think *he's* a cheater and a thief, and he thinks *I* am.

RACHEL: Shh! Someone may be listening!

JACOB: Knowing your father, we can almost count on it.

RACHEL: But you said—

Jacob: Shh! (*Takes her in his arms.*) I was just teasing. There's no one watching us, Rachel. I promise you.

RACHEL: How do you know?

JACOB: My sheep would have told me. Pardon me, your—

RACHEL: —father's sheep, yes. But—but don't you *like* working with my father?

JACOB (*looking at her*):   Now what did my little Rachel mean by that question? (*Stroking his chin.*) If she meant do I enjoy working for crafty old Laban—then *no.* I hate it. There's constant bickering, constant jockeying for position, constant tension. But—if she meant do I enjoy working to buy my little Rachel for my bride—then *yes!* Yes, I love working for Laban, liar though he is. Is *that* what you were asking?

RACHEL: Well . . . (*Smiling a cunning smile.*)

JACOB: Because if it is, then understand this, Rachel. You are worth *far* more to me than seven years of hard work. You're worth my whole life. (*They kiss.*)

LEAH (*enters behind them*):   Rachel—Oh. Sorry. (*They break apart, embarrassed. LEAH's character can be quite funny. She appears to be dumb, speaking in a dull, flat monotone. But she really has more sense than she shows, preferring to hide what she knows.*)

RACHEL (*icy*):   Yes, Sister?

LEAH: Mother wants you.

RACHEL: What for?

LEAH: I don't know.

RACHEL: She didn't tell you?

LEAH: She didn't tell me, and I didn't ask.

RACHEL: Thanks a lot. (*Starts off.*)

LEAH: Anytime I can be of service.

RACHEL: I'll be back. (*She exits; LEAH watches her off. JACOB sits, watches his sheep. LEAH looks back at JACOB. We can see that she likes him, too.*)

LEAH: You—ah—you hungry or anything?

JACOB: No.

LEAH: Thirsty?

JACOB (*smiles*): No, thanks.

LEAH: I think I'll sit out here for a minute.

JACOB: Fine. (LEAH *looks at* JACOB; JACOB *looks at sheep.*) Well, what's the news, Sis? The old man found you a husband yet?

LEAH: I don't know. Maybe. He says he has something up his sleeve.

JACOB: That's your father, all right. He's *always* got something up his sleeve.

LEAH (*smiling*): That's funny. He says that about you.

(JACOB *smiles at that.*) You've been with us almost seven years now, haven't you?

JACOB: Yep. Almost done my time.

LEAH: Where will you go after you and—after you—get married?

JACOB: I don't know. I can't go back home to Canaan.

LEAH: Why?

JACOB: My older brother would put an arrow through me! We didn't exactly part friends.

LEAH: Then . . . maybe . . . you would stay?

JACOB: Stay around Laban? No way! The only thing that could keep me here is Rachel, and she'll soon be mine.

LEAH: I'd better get back to the tents. (*Starts off, stops.*) I—I hope you won't be disappointed, Jacob.

JACOB: Disappointed? Me? Couldn't happen, Leah! You see, I've got this agreement with God. He takes care of me, see, and I take care of Him.

LEAH: How?

JACOB: How what?

LEAH: How do you take care of Him?

JACOB: Oh. Well, I worship Him.

LEAH: Oh. I'm sure He's very pleased. (*Exits; blackout.*)

(*Blues dim up;* JACOB *is again with the* ANGEL.)

JACOB: I thought it did please you!

ANGEL: Did you think God could be bought, Jacob? As you would trade for a goat or a robe, did you think you could trade for God?

JACOB: Look, I did my *best*, Lord! You could have done a *little* better by me!

ANGEL: What did Laban do to you that you did not do to your own father?

JACOB: But, Lord! I thought we had a deal!

ANGEL: Consider your life, Jacob. Remember that first wedding night?

JACOB (*moans*): How could I forget? (*Blackout.*)

(*Lights up, blues and pinks.*)

JACOB (*enters slightly tipsy, groping around*): Oh, what a beautiful morning. Fresh air, yellow fields, and a brand new wife. And what a wife. Rachel! Rachel, come on outside! (*Reaches offstage, pulls* LEAH, *who is wearing a veil, into view.*) Ah, my little Rachel. My dove, my lamb, come. (*Embraces her; she cringes.*) Why do you draw back? (*Sniffs.*) Mmmmm! The fragrance of your hair! None was ever so sweet as my tender, my beautiful (*raises the veil, then in shock*) Leah!

LEAH (*falls to her knees, covers head*): Don't hit me!

JACOB: Hit you? I don't want to hit you. Where's my wife? And what are you doing in her wedding dress?

LEAH: It's not *her* dress, it's *my* dress! And she's *not* your wife, I am! (*He stares at her; she covers her head again.*) Don't hit me!

JACOB: But . . . I . . . You . . . Laban . . . He did this to me! Laban! Laban! (*Runs toward exit; LABAN enters to meet him, walking JACOB back toward center stage, unfrightened by JACOB's implied threat.*)

LABAN: Yes, my boy? You called me? Ah, Jacob, my new son-in-law. It's a beautiful bright day, is it not?

JACOB (*has been building a head of steam, now explodes*): You . . . you . . . you cheated me!

LABAN: My! (*Pats his ears in mocking disbelief*): Laban is getting to be an old man. He seemed to hear you call him a . . . a cheat?

JACOB: Yes! Yes, you're a cheat! Is this the way you treat me? Haven't I slaved for you for seven long years for Rachel? And this is how you treat me? (*He is bouncing on his toes in frustration.*)

LABAN (*calmly*): Oh, I hardly call watching a flock of sheep *slavery*, my son. They're such docile creatures. But I do understand how you might be a little upset.

JACOB (*shouts*): Upset? Upset!?

LABAN: Please stop shouting, boy, you'll hurt your voice. (*Slaps his ears.*) Not to mention my ears. Let's be reasonable about this, shall we?

JACOB (*fuming*): You . . . I . . . Leah . . . reasonable?

LABAN: I couldn't very well marry my younger girl to you while the older daughter is still without a husband. It would bring dishonor to my eldest girl. So let me remind you of the specific terms of our contract. You agreed to labor with me seven years to marry my daughter. It's done! There she is. (*Points to LEAH.*)

LEAH: Please don't hit me. . . .

JACOB: Would you quit saying that! Laban, she's not the right one! You know that!

LABAN: She's not? Oh. Well, now, let me see. Seven years of labor seems to be a good price for a daughter. Now, Rachel is a skinny little thing, I realize, but suppose you spend the marriage week with this one, and then I'll give you Rachel . . .

JACOB: Done!

LABAN: . . . at the price of another seven years.

JACOB: Oh. (*He looks at* LEAH, *back at* LABAN, *then sits on the ground and pantomimes covering his head with dirt.*)

LABAN (*shaking his head and brushing the pantomimed dust away*):   The things young men will do for love. Well, don't mourn too long, my son. Get this wife business taken care of so that we can get back to the *serious* things of life. Like making money! (*Exits; blackout.*)

JACOB (*in the darkness*):   For twenty years I labored for Laban. I personally replaced all of his losses, and his herd grew. Heat wore me down by day and cold by night, and I lost much sleep. Ten times that man changed my wages! (*Lights dim up to blue;* ANGEL *and* JACOB *struggle again.*) I know that had you not been with me, Lord, I would surely have left Laban's house emptyhanded. But you saw my misery, and my labor. I guess—I guess you *have* blessed me.

ANGEL: Then why do you wrestle, Jacob? What are you wrestling for? You have wives, twelve strong children, great herds of sheep and goats—why do you struggle, Jacob? What do you still crave?

JACOB: I . . . I don't know. Forgiveness, perhaps? Safety for my wives and children? A place to *be* . . . and. . . .

ANGEL: And what, Jacob.

JACOB: . . . and . . . and peace. Peace between you and me.

ANGEL: If you seek God's peace, Jacob, it will cost you more than your questionable "worship." It will cost you your life, Jacob.

JACOB: My life? You mean I must *die* to find peace?

ANGEL: I did not say it would cost you your death, Jacob. I said it would cost your *life*.

JACOB: But . . . But I've given you my life—

ANGEL: No. You've given a *part* of yourself. You made an altar to God and called it "God's house." You came to "God's house" to say your prayers and perform your rituals. But God is not satisfied with sacrifices of rams and burnt offerings. A clean heart is God's joy. A broken and penitent heart God will not despise.

JACOB: Penitent? You mean . . . sorry for sin?

ANGEL: You've come to God's house, Jacob. But you have yet to meet Him face to face.

JACOB: But—then—who are *you?* And how do I really meet *Him?*

ANGEL: Do you really want to, Jacob?

JACOB: Yes! I told you, I want peace . . . forgiveness!

ANGEL: Then face yourself, Jacob. Face your sin.

JACOB: My—my sin—

ANGEL: What is your name?

JACOB: What's—why, you know what my name is—

ANGEL: What is your name, and what does it mean?

JACOB: Oh—yes. Yes. My name is Jacob. Jacob—the cheat.

ANGEL: And are you?

JACOB (*looking up*): Yes. Yes, I'm a cheat. I've cheated my father ... I cheated my brother. I cheated my uncle Laban. But—most of all, I realize now—I cheated myself.

ANGEL: And?

JACOB: And I want to be different. I want to meet God, face to face.

ANGEL: *Now* I can bless you, one formerly called the Cheat. For no longer will your name be Jacob. From now on your name is Israel, meaning "he who strives with God"! For you have wrestled with God, and wrestled with your own sin, and have emerged victorious through your own repentance. This is how you win blessing from me, O Israel—you and the tribe that will bear your name—by repentance. And you shall continue to be blessed of God, for out of your seed will come one through whom all nations will be able to receive forgiveness. Go, Israel. You are a new man with a new name, and a new dawn breaks over the eastern hills.

JACOB: Wait, I—Ohhhh! My hip! It's—it's out of joint!

ANGEL: And if there ever should come a time when you doubt this meeting took place, your hip will remind you. When a man wrestles with the Lord, he cannot help but limp away—a very different person.

JACOB: But—but what is your name! Who are you, you who speak for God?

ANGEL: Why do you need to know? Your name is Israel, and God is with you. What other knowledge do you need? (AN-GEL *exits, lights are dimming up to bright.*)

JACOB: It's—it's dawn. I've been at this all night. And Esau will be—Esau. Lord! What about Esau! I—I . . . I must believe. (*Gets up, winces.*) Ohh! (*Grasps his hip.*) I *must* believe. He *is* with me. I've met *God* face to face . . . and He is *with* me—

RACHEL (*enters with* LEAH *behind her*): Jacob! Jacob, he's coming, Esau, your brother! Get up!

LEAH: What's the matter, husband? You're limping. . . .

JACOB: Rachel, Leah, my wives—I'm—I'm all right.

RACHEL: Esau is coming, with four hundred men!

JACOB: Shh! It's all right. God is with me. (ESAU *enters.*) Esau. (RACHEL *and* LEAH *both look at* JACOB, *and he nods. They both bow low to the ground.*)

ESAU: Jacob. (*Now* JACOB *falls to his knees, wincing but determined to bow also.*) Jacob, no! (ESAU *runs to grab him, lifts him to his feet.*) My beloved brother! (*He embraces* JACOB, *who is very surprised.*)

JACOB: Esau? You welcome me with open arms?

ESAU: Well, of course I do! Welcome home, brother! What were all of those herds of sheep and cattle I met on the way?

JACOB: They—they're gifts, to gain my master's favor. . . .

ESAU: Your master? Oh, you mean me? No, keep them, Jacob. I have plenty.

JACOB: No, please! You will honor me if you accept my present, for . . . for being in your presence is like being in the presence of God!

ESAU: Oh, come now, Jacob. What about me is anything like God?

JACOB: Your . . . forgiveness, Esau. Your loving forgiveness.

ESAU: Come on! I have supper waiting for you! (*They put their arms around one another's shoulders and exit*, RACHEL *and* LEAH *following*.)

(*The play can be finished here with a blackout, or if you wish to move to an invitation the following may be added: The* ANGEL *reappears on the opposite side of the stage from the group exit and speaks to the audience.*)

ANGEL: The *face* of God. That's what Jacob . . . what Israel named this place of wrestling. Here in the midst of great inner struggle he found the one thing he had been seeking all of his life—peace and forgiveness from God. But what about you? Are you wrestling tonight? Are you trying to make a deal with God? You can come to his house . . . you can call it worship . . . but you'll never find peace until you *meet* God, face to face.

God Appointed a Worm

A One-Act Play About Jonah

I love the title. My wife and I had been appointed as missionaries—it was my second tour overseas. I was miserable. The weather was always hot, nothing ever worked, missionary morale was chronically low—so I turned to the story of Jonah for inspiration. What I discovered was that I had a "worm's-eye-view" of my own calling. I wasn't seeing the world through God's eyes, but—like Jonah—I was seeing the faults of others around me and wishing God would *do* something about them. Through the writing of the play I realized: How can we minister to people if we don't love them? And how can we love them if we don't let God change our viewpoint? Jonah learned that. If we as Christians are to care enough about the world to want to win them to Jesus Christ, *we* need to learn it anew.

Cast of Characters

3 women, 3 men

Women: Narrator

           Messenger/Crowd 2

           Sailor/Crowd 3

Men: Jonah

           Captain/Crowd 1/Herald

           Mate/King/Worm

Setting

All over the ancient world!

The setting of this play shifts quickly several times—from a stage, to Judah, to the deck of a ship, to the belly of a fish, etc., thus the set ought to be capable of suggesting many different places easily. The platform of a church does nicely, since there are usually several "levels" already in place, and the backdrop suggests universal themes. If the resources are available, however, the author suggests that a four-foot level with an attached stair unit be placed up left, with a chair nearby for JONAH to carry up with him when he ascends the platform. The platform or level needs to be large enough to accommodate three players at one time. Down right, the author suggests there be a construction of wood, wire hoops, and netting, preferably fishnet. During the "ship" scene, this would look appropriate for the deck. When JONAH is tossed overboard, he would crawl within the netting. This contraption ought to be constructed so that pulling one rope off left would raise the metal hoops within the netting, creating a tube of net around JONAH. Lighted from within or from behind, this can give an interesting "belly of the fish" effect. None of the above is necessary, however. The play was written to be taken on tour by a small cast, and the fewer the props and set pieces, the better.

(At rise we see a four-foot level up left with a stair unit up to it. Down right is a pile of what looks like fishnet. NARRATOR —a woman—enters and walks down center to address the audience.)

NARRATOR: Good evening. We're about to tell you a story that may already be familiar to you. It's about a man named Jonah, who was called by God to be a missionary. Most people call the story "Jonah and the Whale," but the title of this play is "God appointed a worm—"

JONAH (*entering, angrily shaking his script*):   I heard that!

NARRATOR (*whispering*): Jonah, go back, this isn't your cue—

JONAH: I don't care. I just want you and them (*pointing to audience*) to know how much that title offends me!

NARRATOR: Jonah, would you please—

JONAH: Look what you've said! You've already told these people this is a play about missions, and what do you do to missionaries, hmm?

NARRATOR: I don't know, what *do* you do to missionaries?

JONAH: You appoint them!

NARRATOR: Well?

JONAH: That title's going to make them all think *I'm* the worm!

NARRATOR (*aside*): It certainly will now, for sure.

JONAH: In fact, I don't like anything about this play! The whole script seems calculated to say that I do nothing but complain!

NARRATOR: Well . . .

JONAH: Well what!

NARRATOR: What are you doing now?

JONAH (*understanding, then angry*): Listen, I've got a right to complain! In fact, I want you to tell the director that I'm doing this whole play under protest!

NARRATOR: I'm sure he already knows.

JONAH (*was starting off, now stops and comes back*):   What do you mean by that?

NARRATOR: Well, it's hardly a surprise, is it? You remember what you said when the Lord first told you to go to Nineveh? (*She takes his script and starts off right as* MESSENGER, *another woman, enters left.*)

MESSENGER: Jonah, son of Amitai? (*Am/e/tie*)

Jonah (*after* NARRATOR):   I told you I didn't want to do this play!

NARRATOR (*stops and looks back*):   It's *your* life story, Jonah, remember? Answer God's messenger. (*She exits.*)

MESSENGER: Excuse me, but are you—

JONAH: Yes, I'm Jonah. What do you want?

MESSENGER: The Lord has sent me to give you a message.

JONAH: The Lord?

MESSENGER: Pack your bags and go to the great city of Nineveh.

JONAH: Nineveh!

MESSENGER: Tell them that God has seen their wickedness, and He's angry.

JONAH: Nineveh? The capital of Assyria?

MESSENGER: Tell them that in forty days God will destroy the city.

JONAH: Have you ever *seen* any Assyrians? Those people are *mean!*

MESSENGER: You're to go to Nineveh, Jonah. That's the word of the Lord.

JONAH: They've got iron swords! They file their teeth into little points!

MESSENGER: Go to Nineveh, Jonah.

JONAH: They'll eat me for supper!

MESSENGER: I'm just telling you what God said to—

JONAH: How do I know you're from God? (*Suspiciously.*) You got any identification?

MESSENGER: Search your heart, Jonah.

JONAH: I'd really rather not . . .

MESSENGER: Because you know I'm speaking the truth.

JONAH: I've got an idea! Why don't *you* go!

MESSENGER: The Lord is sending *you.*

JONAH: I'd better pack. (*Pantomimes packing.*)

MESSENGER (*surprised*): You mean you're going after all?

JONAH: Well, I'm sure not staying here! And there's a ship leaving for Joppa tomorrow morning.

MESSENGER: I'm . . . I'm a little surprised. It sounded like you were going to refuse. (JONAH *is exiting right.*) But wait! You can't get to Nineveh by ship!

JONAH (*turning around*): You think *I* don't know that? (*Blackout.*) (*Lights up to reveal* CAPTAIN, MATE, *and* SAILOR. *All wear sick looks and sway from side to side in* unison, as if rocked by a boat. They're calling to one another, as if above the sounds of a storm. Optional sound effect: storm winds.)

CAPTAIN: Look over there! You see a break in the clouds?

MATE (hand to forehead, peering over audience):   I don't see none, Cap'n!

CAPTAIN: Nor do I! We'd better keep praying!

SAILOR: Better hurry, Cap'n! She'll soon start breaking up!

CAPTAIN: Who have we prayed to so far?

MATE: Let's see: Zeus, Baal, Poseidon, Dagon, Ishtar, Osiris— You want me to read the whole list?

CAPTAIN: Just tell me who we've skipped!

MATE: I can't think of any!

SAILOR: What about Jonah's God?

CAPTAIN: Who?

SAILOR: Jonah! That Jew!

CAPTAIN: Who's his god? I'll pray to anybody!

SAILOR: He didn't say the name! Just that he was running away from him!

CAPTAIN: Then find Jonah and ask him!

MATE: Where is he, anyway?

SAILOR: He was sick last time I saw him! Jonah? Jonah! (Exits right.)

MATE: Did he fall over the side?

CAPTAIN: He better *not* have. I need the name of his god!

SAILOR (*offstage*):   He's down here! (*Leading a sick-looking* JONAH *onstage.*) He was asleep!

CAPTAIN: Asleep! How can you sleep when we're all about to drown?

JONAH (*holding stomach*):   It seemed better than being sick . . .

CAPTAIN: Hurry! Call upon your god! Perhaps he'll listen to you, and spare us all!

JONAH: Ah . . . I wouldn't count on that too much if I were you—

MATE: Captain! We'll soon be lost! Let's cast lots to find out who it is the gods hate!

CAPTAIN: Right! (CAPTAIN, MATE, *and* SAILOR *all drop to knees.* JONAH *remains standing, swaying from side to side and holding stomach.* CAPTAIN *rolls dice.*) Ha! It isn't me!

MATE (*rolls, nervously*):   Look! Not me either!

SAILOR (*rolls, claps hands*):   It ain't me!

CAPTAIN: Jonah! You roll!

JONAH: I'd really rather not—(CAPTAIN *and* MATE *jerk* JONAH *to his knees and hand him dice. He rolls—all three gaze at him in horror.*) (*Pause.*) Did I lose?

CAPTAIN: What have you done, to bring this evil upon us!

MATE: Where are you from!

SAILOR: And who's this god who's showed us his anger and his might!

JONAH: I am Jonah, son of Amitai. I'm a Hebrew, and I fear the Lord, who made heaven and earth and the sea.

CAPTAIN: I fear Him too! I fear He's about to sink us!

MATE: What evil have you done?

JONAH: He told me to go to Nineveh!

SAILOR: Nineveh! But those people are *mean!*

JONAH: That's what I said.

MATE: You can't get to Nineveh by ship!

JONAH: I said that, too . . .

CAPTAIN: What shall we do to you, to calm this raging tempest?

JONAH: Truly this is all my fault! (*Grandly.*) Take me and hurl me into the sea, and the Lord will make it calm for you! (*Nervously.*) Of course, if you'd rather not, I'll be happy to help bail—

CAPTAIN: Throw you overboard? Never!

MATE: We wouldn't think of it!

SAILOR: Why, it wouldn't be decent! (*Pause.*) (MATE *and* SAILOR *suddenly grab* JONAH *by hands and legs, head downstage, as* CAPTAIN *clasps hands together and raises pious eyes to heaven.*)

CAPTAIN: Oh Lord, we beseech you! Let us not perish for this man's life, and please don't hate us! He told us to do it, and we have done it only to please you! Amen. (*To sailors.*) Toss him!

MATE/SAILOR: One! Two! Three!

JONAH: Ahh! (*Blackout. Sound: splash.*) (*Spotlight up on* JONAH, *or lights within the "fishnet"—see Author's Note.* JONAH *is lying on his face. Gradually he pushes himself up to his hands.*)

JONAH: Am I dead? Is this the grave? (*He sits, feels of self.*) I . . . I'm not a ghost . . . not a shade . . . I can still feel . . . (*Sniffs—makes a face.*) I can still smell! Whew! Never expected the grave to smell like tunafish! The ground is— no, it's not ground! It's all wet, and slimy . . . it's so dark . . . where am I?

NARRATOR: You're inside a fish, Jonah.

JONAH (*frightened*): Who's there! (*Pause, uncertainly.*) You can't be God; you're a woman.

NARRATOR: God often speaks through women, Jonah—especially where missions is concerned.

JONAH: What's missions?

NARRATOR: It's being sent by God to do a task—like you were, Jonah.

JONAH: How do you know about that!

NARRATOR: I told you, Jonah, I'm God's messenger.

JONAH: If you're God's messenger, why don't *you* go to Nineveh?

NARRATOR: Because it's *you* God's appointed for that task. You've been specially selected to go.

JONAH: But why me!

NARRATOR: Why not you?

JONAH: I can think of plenty of reasons! For one thing, I hate Assyrians!

NARRATOR: You've never met an Assyrian.

JONAH: How do you know that! Oh, right. I keep forgetting.

NARRATOR: Like many men, you're afraid of what you've never seen.

JONAH: Well, wouldn't you be?

NARRATOR: Not if I knew God was with me.

JONAH (*sarcastically*): I suppose I'm gonna meet the Lord in the middle of a pack of howling Assyrian murderers?

NARRATOR: If God met you in the belly of a fish, where He did *not* send you—don't you think He'll meet you in Nineveh, where He *did?*

JONAH: I'm really in the belly of a fish?

NARRATOR: That's right.

JONAH: Must be a mighty big fish!

NARRATOR: Specially prepared by God.

JONAH: Just to swallow me?

NARRATOR: Who can know all of God's purposes, even for

something as simple as a fish? The Lord is infinitely creative. Today this creature is your salvation from the sea. Tomorrow it may feed a starving village. God does what He chooses. And sometimes, He lets us help Him do it.

JONAH: How long have I been in here?

NARRATOR (*with meaning*): Three days, Jonah, and three long nights.

JONAH: You say that so purposefully—is there something significant about that period of time?

NARRATOR: There will be, one day. Something very significant.

JONAH: Am . . . am I ever going to get out?

NARRATOR: The Lord didn't save you for nothing.

JONAH: Then . . . He . . . heard my prayers? In spite of my running from Him?

NARRATOR: You can't run so far from God that He cannot hear your call for help.

JONAH: I . . . did call. As I went beneath the waves, and the ship rolled over me, I was sure I'd never see the surface again. In that moment—strange, but the one thing I wanted to see was the temple, glistening in the sunlight atop Mount Zion. And I cried out to God. Oh, I had the good sense not to open my mouth underwater; but I prayed, nevertheless. And then it seemed like the water weeds grabbed me around the head, trying to pull me further under. I was lost then, and I knew it. I committed my soul to the one I'd run away from . . . (*Pause.*)

NARRATOR (*kindly*): What's the matter?

JONAH: I'm ashamed. I don't deserve salvation.

NARRATOR: None of us do, Jonah. But God keeps giving it anyway. Hold on. You're about to come back out onto dry land.

JONAH (*excited*):   Really? Right now?

NARRATOR: Better contain your excitement. You may not like how you get there. (*Blackout, then up on general lighting.* JONAH *lies on his face on top of the fish net.*)

JONAH (*stands up slowly, making a face, then shakes his arms*): Yuck!

NARRATOR: Well, how else were you going to get out?

JONAH: I've heard of men getting sick from eating fish, but never the other way around!

NARRATOR: When you air out a little, better start walking. Nineveh is that way, and it's a long walk.

JONAH: You mean I'm not there yet?

NARRATOR: If you can't get there by ship, Jonah, you sure can't get there by fish! Start walking! (*Blackout.*)

JONAH (*lights up and we see* JONAH *center stage*):   People of Nineveh! Hear my voice! I am a messenger, sent by God! The Lord, who made heaven and earth, has seen your wicked deeds! He's seen your armies oppress the weaker nations and watched you revel in your savage triumphs! And the wrath of the Lord blows hot upon Nineveh! I've been sent to proclaim it! Forty days is all you have to finish the business of living! Forty days to close your affairs, because that's when this city will be destroyed! Hear my message, you Assyrian murderers! Hear and tremble before

God! (*A crowd of three has gathered before the apron of the stage, and they murmur together anxiously.*)

CROWD 1(m):   We'll utterly be destroyed?

CROWD 2(f):   Is this god going to kill us all?

JONAH: The Lord has promised total destruction! No more will the world tremble at the clash of your iron swords!

CROWD 3(f):   What if we repent? What happens then?

JONAH: Why . . . nothing will change! I hope. I mean, the Lord has made up His mind! Nineveh is doomed to destruction!

CROWD 3:   Couldn't you plead with your god on our behalf?

JONAH: What? Me plead for you? Forget it!

CROWD 2:   The king must hear of this! Right now! (*Races off.*)

JONAH (*pointing after her*):   Won't do him any good! He'll fry, just like the rest of you! (*Crowd exits, talking anxiously.*) (*Chuckles, rubs hands together in a bloodthirsty way.*) (*To himself.*) You know, this could get to be fun! (*Blackout.*)

CROWD 2:   My lord! My lord!

KING: What? What is it?

CROWD 2 (*bows to the floor*):   Oh king, live forever—I have threatening news! There's a preacher in the city square who says Nineveh's going to be destroyed!

KING: Preachers are always talking about destruction.

CROWD 2:   My lord King, this one is different!

KING: How is he different? Is he dressed strangely?

CROWD 2:   No . . . though he does smell a bit . . .

KING: Is his message any different?

CROWD 2:   Not really. Standard prophecy of doom with a time limit on it . . .

KING: Then what's different about him?

CROWD 2:   There's . . . there's something *with* him—or some-*one* . . .

KING (*alarmed*):   Yes?

CROWD 2:   But the biggest difference is the burning his message began in my heart. (*Seriously, looking* KING *in the face.*) My lord—I believe him. (*They freeze—slow fade to black.*)

(*Lights up, and* JONAH *is back center stage.*)

JONAH: People of Nineveh, listen to me! Your city, your nation is doomed! The whole nation shall—(*he breaks off, as* HERALD *enters, stands next to him, and unrolls scroll.*) Ah, excuse me, but I'm working this particular corner—

HERALD: Hear ye, hear ye! (NARRATOR *enters to listen.*) By order of the King! We have heard the word of destruction, and we believe! Let neither man nor beast, herd nor flock taste anything! Let man and beast be covered with sackcloth, and let them cry mightily to God! Let every man turn from his violence and wickedness. Who knows, God may yet repent and turn from His fierce anger, and we won't perish! (*He rolls up scroll and exits.* JONAH *stares after him, perplexed.*)

NARRATOR: You've done your job well, Jonah. You can go home.

JONAH: Go home? Not on your life! I want to wait around and watch the fireworks!

NARRATOR: There aren't going to be any fireworks.

JONAH: Of course there are! God's going to rain down fire and brimstone like He did on Sodom and Gomorrah! That's the message He told me to preach—

NARRATOR: And the people received it. He's changed his mind, Jonah. He's not going to destroy the city after all.

JONAH (*pause—then angry*):   I knew it! I knew it! Way back *home* I knew it! I get all the way up here, preach myself blue in the face, make an absolute idiot of myself for God—then He backs out. Oh, I knew you'd do it, God! (*Shaking fist at the sky.*)

NARRATOR: That makes you angry?

JONAH: Of course it makes me angry! In six weeks you know what these people are gonna be saying? "Whatever happened to that smelly prophet Jonah? He sure made a fool of himself!"

NARRATOR: But Jonah, God's purpose all along was for Nineveh to repent! That's why He sent you.

JONAH: I know that! He's a gracious and merciful God, slow to anger, and quick to forgive! I *knew* He wouldn't come through! (*He starts off.*)

NARRATOR: Where are you going?

JONAH: I'm going up on that mountain to wait. These wicked Assyrians can't keep out of trouble for a whole month! And when they stumble again, maybe God'll lose His temper and fry them after all! (*Exits.*)

NARRATOR (*to herself*):   Oh, Jonah. If God saved only the worthy, where would that leave you and me? (*Blackout.*)

(*Lights up revealing* JONAH *sitting on platform on a chair, his arms folded, surveying the audience sternly. Behind him crouches* PLANT.) (*Pause.*)

JONAH: I'm waiting. (*Pause.*) Come on, Lord, you *know* they're not *all* fasting and praying! Somebody down there is sneaking a quick snack! (PLANT *"grows" behind him.*) Just remember who these people are, Lord! (*Pause.*) Whew! Is it hot. (*Pause.*) Think about what they've done! You can't mean you're going to let them get away with it—(*He notices* PLANT *and jumps up, startled.*) Ah! Who are you!

PLANT: I'm a plant.

JONAH: A plant! You weren't there when I sat down! A plant can't grow that fast!

PLANT: I did.

JONAH: But I don't understand! How?

PLANT: The Lord saw you seated here under the hot sun. God appointed me to grow up over you, to shade you from the heat.

JONAH: God did that? For me?

PLANT (*stretching arms over him*):   There. Is that all right?

JONAH: That's great! Well, maybe a little to the left . . . (PLANT *adjusts.*) There. Just right. (*He settles back in his chair and sighs.*) This is living!

WORM   (*enters, below platform*):   Are you Jonah, son of Amitai?

JONAH: Oh, no. Who are you, another messenger of God?

WORM: I guess so, in a way. I'm a worm.

JONAH: You? You're the worm?

WORM: That's right.

JONAH: And God appointed you?

WORM: Right again.

JONAH (*laughs and claps his hands*):   And all the time I thought *I* was the worm!

WORM: What's wrong with being a worm?

JONAH: Why, don't you know?

WORM: No.

JONAH: Well . . . nobody wants to be a worm!

WORM: I do. I like being a worm.

JONAH: You do?

WORM: Of course. But I'm not just a worm. I'm a worm appointed by God. I may be small and insignificant to a human being, but the Lord has a purpose for me. (*He is climbing up the platform steps, as the plant cowers in terror.*)

JONAH: What is your purpose, anyway?

WORM: I'm here to eat the plant.

JONAH: To eat my plant! Don't you dare eat my plant!

WORM: It isn't your plant; it's God's plant, and He sent me to attack it. (WORM *seizes* PLANT *by the neck; she rolls her eyes, gasps, and withers as* JONAH *shouts.*)

JONAH: Stop that! Quit! Leave her alone! Stop—(JONAH *is trying to pry worm's fingers free. As they struggle, the* PLANT *"dies," rolling head to chest and dropping arms.* JONAH *gazes wrathfully at* WORM, *shouts.*) You *worm!* (JONAH *stomps his foot.* WORM, *too, "dies."*) Look at my beautiful shade! She's withered! And the hot sun! The heat . . . all right, God! (*Shaking fist at the sky.*) Why don't you just go ahead and kill me! You've done everything else to me! (NARRATOR *enters, below platform.*) Getting me tossed into the sea—

NARRATOR: I thought that was your suggestion.

JONAH: Having me swallowed by a fish—

NARRATOR: Which saved your life, remember?

JONAH: And having the fish throw me up on the shore!

NARRATOR: You said you wanted out . . .

JONAH: Making me preach destruction to a nation of murderers!

NARRATOR: Who treated you very kindly and listened to your message.

JONAH: And then made a fool of me by accepting their repentance!

NARRATOR: Just like He accepted yours from the belly of the fish.

JONAH (*still looking up*):   Now you play this cruel joke on me, giving me a beautiful plant for shade—

NARRATOR: Which grew in a moment purely by God's grace—

JONAH: And then destroying it with a slimy, loathesome worm!

NARRATOR: Which really only acted like you're acting now.

JONAH (*for the first time looks down at* NARRATOR):   What did you say?

NARRATOR: You're acting just like the worm. It attacked another of God's creatures to destroy it, just like you're attacking Nineveh.

JONAH (*protesting, coming off the platform*):   Now wait a minute! I didn't attack Nineveh; I just did what God told me to do!

NARRATOR: Finally. But didn't you attack Nineveh when you first refused to warn the city of God's wrath?

JONAH (*defensively*):   Well . . .

NARRATOR: And aren't you still attacking when you plead with God to destroy her, despite her repentant spirit?

JONAH (*weakening*):   Well . . .

NARRATOR: You pity the plant, for which you didn't labor, which lived and died in the purpose of God. Then shouldn't the Lord pity Nineveh, in which are a hundred and twenty thousand people that He made—and loves?

JONAH: Well. (*Pause. Gazes out at the audience, at "Nineveh."*) I guess . . . I guess I've just had a worm's-eye view of the world. And the Lord's been trying to help me see it from His perspective.

NARRATOR: And what do you see, looking at it all through God's eyes?

JONAH (*pause*):   I see people. People beloved of God, who are running from Him as I did. I see people He's appointed to various tasks, who are asleep in the bottom of the boat. I see people who are drowning in the waters of sin, who are crying out for salvation. I see people pointing accusing fingers at the wicked, secretly hoping their words won't be heard, so that they can feel more self-righteous. And I see people—so many "good" people, just sitting—waiting for the destruction of the rest of the world, all the time railing at God for not making them feel more comfortable. I see all of this—and it makes me feel more like a worm than ever.

NARRATOR: Don't be so hard on yourself, Jonah. For perhaps your story—and your willingness to tell it—can help some of those out there to get a God's-eye view of their own.

An Eclipse of the Son

A One-Act Parable of Spiritual Blindness

This is an Easter play, of sorts. It is not, however, a passion play—at least, not about the passion of Christ. It *does* reveal how our petty passions often obscure our vision, preventing us from seeing what is really important. Although this day is set in the time of Christ, Jacob and Joseph are not biblical characters. Because that's so, they need not be taken so seriously. The humor at the beginning of the play, which borders on slapstick, sets up the tragic nature of Jacob's final condition. Through it all, literally in the background, the events of our Lord's passion unfold—unnoticed by the principal character. Isn't that how so many people in the world live? The gospel is ever present, there in the background of their lives, but they never seem to turn around and give attention to it. Perhaps this play could catch the attention of some of those, and help them to look at the Son of God.

Cast of Characters

3 men, 1 woman, several walk-ons

JACOB, An elderly Hebrew

REUBEN, his best friend

MYRA, Jacob's wife

JESUS (This role has only one line)

As many walk-ons as desired

Setting

Jerusalem on the day Christ died.

(JACOB, *a little old man, enters left. He is hunched over, carrying a small table on which are several scrolls of paper—his star charts. He sets it down center and exits, humming. He immediately reenters with a stool, puzzles over where to put it, finally sets it down, sits on it, smiles, and looks to the sky.*)

MYRA (*a rough, shrewish woman with a harsh voice, calls from off left*):   All right! Who took my table outta here!?

JACOB (*face falls, he mutters, mocking her*):   "All right. Who took my table outta here?"

MYRA: Jacob! Where is my table?

JACOB (*mocking*):   "Jacob! Where is my table—" (MYRA *has entered behind him, stands now with hands on hips.*)

MYRA: What!?

JACOB (*startled*):   Oh! Why it's, ah, it's right here, dear. Sitting right here. (*She comes over to glare at him. He points timidly.*) Right here?

MYRA: Gimme that! (*She grabs it; papers go flying; she starts off with it, stops.*) Oh, I see you got the stool, too! Well, bring it along!

JACOB: I'm just—

MYRA: What good's it do me to clean house with you around, you bumbling old fool!

JACOB: I'm just going to sit out here and watch—

MYRA: You're going to bring it along!

JACOB: I'm going to bring the stool along, yes, dear. I'm right behind you . . . (*He picks up stool and starts to follow her off left, but as she exits he makes a little circle back to where he started, puts stool down, sits, and shades his eyes.*) Humph. (REUBEN *enters, smiles, and crosses to* JACOB'*s side.*) Lemme see, if Venus were five degrees west of the sun, then . . . no, no, no, that isn't right. It was east of the sun, Venus was east of the sun, I remember that distinctly. . . .

REUBEN: Jacob! (*He throws his arms wide to welcome his old friend—who pays no attention, but keeps staring up.*)

JACOB: That means Mars must be . . . no, no, no! I'm confusing myself! I've gotta quit (*hitting side of his head with his hand*) doing that. Jacob, you gotta quit it. Now lemme see. . . .

REUBEN: Jacob?

JACOB: Must have messed up somewhere. But I thought I had it right! Where are those charts? I've gotta find that chart. (*He scrambles down on hands and knees, circling* REUBEN *as he scoops up papers, sits, unrolls a scroll, looks up.*) Must be . . . no, if Venus were over there, then. . . .

REUBEN: Jacob!

JACOB (*yelling off toward* MYRA): If you want your stool, you'll have to take it out from under me! (*Smiles to himself.*) Told her, I did! Where was I? Oh yes, if Venus. . . .

REUBEN (*puts hand on* JACOB'*s shoulder, also looks up*):
What, ah—what are you looking at?

JACOB: Huh? (*Not looking at* REUBEN.) Why, stars, of
course! (*Keeps mumbling to himself.*)

REUBEN (*doutbfully*): Stars?

JACOB (*nods sagely*): Stars.

REUBEN (*looking up again*): But it's broad daylight!

JACOB (*cutting him off*): Shh! They're very hard to see. But
it's possible. (*Keeps scanning the sky.*)

REUBEN: Jacob? Remember me?

JACOB: Huh? Why, Reuben! Why didn't you tell me you were
standing there?

REUBEN: Well, I tried—

JACOB: Look here. See? See up there? That's where they are,
Reuben. Up there.

REUBEN: Oh. Stars?

JACOB (*nods sagely, as before*): Stars.

REUBEN: Jacob, you mean to tell me you can see them up
there?

JACOB: What? Why, of course, anyone can see—

REUBEN: In the middle of the day?

JACOB: Well, I confess, it is hard—

REUBEN: Have *you* ever seen a star in the daytime, Jacob?

JACOB: Well, no, but. . . .

REUBEN: But what?

JACOB: But I have faith. (*Still looking up.*)

REUBEN: How's your wife? (JACOB *falls off his stool.*)

JACOB (*getting up, angry*): Why'd you have to bring *her* up!?

REUBEN: Seemed the only way I could get your attention. Jacob!

Jacob: Reuben! (*They throw their arms around each other, then both dissolve into coughing fits.* JACOB *begins dusting himself off—the dust flies from his coat, since it has been liberally powdered before his coming onstage.*) A bit dusty, this street.

REUBEN: What are you doing, sitting out in the middle of the roadway like this? You could get run over by a chariot!

JACOB: Worse. I could get run over by my wife.

REUBEN: Answer my question!

JACOB: I told you, I'm looking—

REUBEN: Besides looking at stars! What's going on with you, Jacob?

JACOB (*joyfully*): Today's the day, Reuben! I just know it!

REUBEN (*happy with him*): Wonderful! The day for what?

JACOB (*stops smiling*): I don't know. But today's the day for it. The stars said so.

REUBEN: Oh, they talk too, do they?

JACOB (*sagely*):   In secret ways. (*Waves him closer, stage whisper.*) The stars hold all the secrets of the world!

REUBEN: Really?

JACOB: Shh! Not so loud. She might hear. Then she'd come out and call me a senile old fool and drag me into the house. Keep it very quiet. (REUBEN *nods, as a man walks on from left and exits right, upstage of them.* JACOB *notices him, but goes on.*) All of mankind's secrets are locked in the stars. To know their motion is to know your own!

REUBEN: I see. And do you know their motion?

JACOB: Shh! I'm learning. Bit by bit, I'm learning. (*Another extra, in costume, crosses from off left to off right.*)

REUBEN (*watching the man cross*):   Can they tell you anything about me?

JACOB: Huh? Why, of course! When were you born?

REUBEN: I don't know. Does it matter?

JACOB (*loudly*):   Oh, tremendously!

REUBEN (*points off left, toward* MYRA):   Shh!

Jacob: Oh. (*Quieter.*) Tremendously.

REUBEN: I thought you said they know all mankind's secrets!

JACOB: Oh, they do!

REUBEN: Then ask them when my birthday was! (*Another person passes from left to right.*)

JACOB: Where are all these people going?

REUBEN: That's what I came over to tell you about. There's going to be a crucifixion today. You want to come along with me?

JACOB: Me, go to a crucifixion? I'm going to waste my time doing that?

REUBEN: Well, you used to go to them.

JACOB: It's a disgusting sight! Tack a man to a couple of boards and hang him up to die—it's terrible.

REUBEN: But there's nothing else to do

JACOB: There's plenty to do!

REUBEN: Such as?

JACOB: Such as learning about the stars! (*Pause—then curious.*) Who is it?

REUBEN: Who's what?

JACOB: Being crucified!

REUBEN: I thought you weren't interested?

JACOB: I'm just wondering if it's anyone I know.

REUBEN: I don't know any of them. There are three scheduled to die, two thieves and a preacher.

JACOB: Two thieves—and a preacher?

REUBEN: That's right.

JACOB: Why him? What did he do?

REUBEN: Only set the whole countryside on its ear, that's

what! Honestly, Jacob, don't you pay any attention to current events?

JACOB: Of course I do! Why, Reuben, all the current events of mankind are hidden in the stars—

REUBEN   (*together with* JACOB: ". . . in the stars." Yes, you've told me. But have they told you anything about this Jesus fellow?

JACOB: Jesus? (*Checks his papers.*) No.

REUBEN: The whole Sanhedrin is up in arms against him, and they've made Pilate agree to crucify him. Even though he hasn't done a single thing that is against the law! He has all of these followers, see, and they are going to storm up there and take him down!

JACOB: Ahh! Never do it. Too many soldiers.

REUBEN: There's another rumor, too. Some people say this fellow is a god, and that he's going to come right down from the cross, by himself!

JACOB: Really?

REUBEN: That's what they say. Exciting, isn't it!

JACOB: You believe them?

REUBEN: No. But I'm gonna be there anyway, just in case. You want to come?

JACOB: Well—maybe.

REUBEN: Who knows, maybe it's the important thing the stars told you would happen today. By the way, they don't really talk, do they?

JACOB: No, no. It's their positions that speak to the eye.

REUBEN: Oh. Well, I'm going. Are you coming with me?

JACOB: I . . . well. . . .

REUBEN: Look, you can be sure the stars aren't gonna talk to you in the daytime.

JACOB: They do sometimes!

REUBEN: How, when you can't even see them?

JACOB: Sometimes an eclipse occurs—

REUBEN: An eclipse?

JACOB: When the moon blocks out the sun.

REUBEN: The moon! In the daytime?

JACOB: It doesn't happen very often.

REUBEN: I would hope not!

JACOB: Maybe I should stay. . . .

REUBEN: If it doesn't happen very often it isn't likely to happen today. Come on, Jacob!

JACOB: I guess it would be a mathematical near impossibility. Here, sit down. I'll get my coat. (JACOB *exits;* REUBEN *sits.* MYRA *enters immediately, jerks stool from under him, dropping* REUBEN *to the floor. He struggles to get up, but stops. Those who have crossed upstage previously now reenter, surrounding the figure of* JESUS, *robed in white, who drags a cross from right to left. This could be conveyed by slide projectors, on backdrop, if preferred.* JACOB *reenters.*)

JACOB: What are you doing down there? I told you this street was dusty.

REUBEN: Your wife came and took the stool—out from under me.

JACOB: Oh, I knew she got it. (*Rubbing head.*) She hit me with it.

REUBEN (*rises*): The crucifixion party just passed by, on the way up to Golgotha.

JACOB: All three?

REUBEN: No, there was just one. He must have been this Jesus fellow. He didn't look like a thief. (*Looks puzzled.*)

JACOB: What's the matter?

REUBEN: Well, he couldn't even *carry* his cross. How is he going to come down off of it?

JACOB (*shrugs*): You still want to go?

REUBEN: Yes. . . .

JACOB: Now what's the matter?

REUBEN: Hmm? He just didn't look like much, that's all. The way they talked, I thought he would be a giant.

JACOB: Even giants shrink up when they're about to be crucified. Are we going or not?

REUBEN: But he didn't look that way! I mean, he looked like he feared it, but he didn't look like he—feared it. You know what I mean?

JACOB (*sincerely*): No.

REUBEN: Anyway, it was curious. Let's go. (*Lights begin to fade.*)

JACOB (*noticing light change*): What's going . . . ?

REUBEN: Come on, we'll miss it!

JACOB: Wait a minute . . . look! (*He points up.*)

REUBEN: Look where? Come on, Jacob, don't waste time.

JACOB: It's starting!

REUBEN: What is?

JACOB: The eclipse! It's starting! Look up there!

REUBEN: It's too bright. (*Shields eyes.*) I'd rather not.

JACOB: Reuben, that's it! That's what the stars were telling me! An eclipse! You go waste your time if you want. I'm going to watch this! (JACOB *hustles off, returns with stool.*)

REUBEN: Jacob, I don't think you're going to want to miss this. I saw this man's face—this Jesus. It was—different from anything I've ever seen.

JACOB: This is different! An eclipse is different! Go on!

REUBEN: If you're sure—

JACOB: Go on! I've got better things to watch!

REUBEN: All right. (*Exits left.*)

JACOB (*to himself*): An eclipse! But why now? This seems impossible! Of course, I never have been any good with figures—and that's what it is all right! An eclipse of the sun! (*Light is slowly fading, but for a bright spot on* JACOB*'s* *face.*) Yes! It's . . . it's beautiful! (*His face begins to show concern—his eyes appear to strain a bit.*) Such . . . such great brilliance . . . (*worry growing in his voice.*) It's—it's gorgeous . . . it's . . . total . . . (*Light on his face fades to black.*)

JESUS (*offstage, or on microphone, in blackout*): Father, forgive them, for they know not what they do. (*There is silence in the black for a moment; then lights fade back up.*)

REUBEN (*enters, running, breathless*): Jacob! You should have been there! The strangest thing I ever saw! They—

JACOB (*nervously, not looking at him*): Did he—come down?

REUBEN: What? Oh, no, nothing like that. That's just it! I stood there watching him as he died, Jacob, and—I can't explain why but—but I really *expected* him to come down. But he didn't. He just hung there and died. He . . . look, I talked to some of the people around me, women mostly, who have been following him for years. They told me that this man did all kinds of miracles, like he raised a man from the dead just a few weeks ago! Lazarus, a fellow from Bethany. Some of them swore they saw him do it! And—

JACOB: Reuben?

REUBEN: Yes?

JACOB (*trying to laugh*): Did you see the eclipse?

REUBEN: What? Oh. Yeah. Well, I mean I noticed it got dark.

JACOB: Reuben?

REUBEN: What is it, Jacob?

JACOB (*anxiously*): Is it over?

REUBEN (*puzzled*): Is what over? What are you talking about?

JACOB: The eclipse! Is it light again?

REUBEN: Why sure, can't you—

JACOB (*quickly*): This man, you say he raised someone from the dead?

REUBEN (*puzzled, but eager to finish his story*): Yes, and he turned water into wine, and made lame people walk.

JACOB (*quickly*): Did he make the blind see?

REUBEN: Yes . . . Jacob? Is there something wrong?

JACOB: Take me to him! (*He holds his hands out.*) (*Pause.*)

REUBEN: Jacob, he's dead.

JACOB: He's dead? (*Slumps on the stool.*)

REUBEN: Yes. (*Looking away.*) After . . . after being tortured like that—beaten—speared in the side—after all that, he forgave those who were killing him. Strange, huh? (*Pausing.*) Jacob? Are you—blind?

JACOB (*quietly*): I'm afraid so.

REUBEN (*quietly*): Jacob?

JACOB (*quickly*): It doesn't matter.

REUBEN: But your eyes—

JACOB (*angrily*): I said it didn't matter! (*He slumps on the stool. It very evidently does matter.*)

REUBEN: They . . . they said something else.

JACOB: What?

REUBEN: That this man Jesus would rise up again from the dead . . . in three days.

JACOB (*turns his head sightlessly toward* REUBEN):   What?

REUBEN: They said he would be resurrected from the dead in three days. (*Pause.*)

JACOB (*rising*):   Well, then. We'll just have to wait three days.

REUBEN: You mean you believe that?

JACOB: When it suddenly comes clear to you that you're lost in darkness, belief comes rather easy. Yes, I believe them.

REUBEN: But Jacob, how can someone—

JACOB: It appears that I was blinding myself when I should have been looking at Jesus. If what they say is true, perhaps it's not too late to change that. Three days, you say?

REUBEN: That's—what they told me. . . .

JACOB: Why, that isn't so long. Not so long at all. Help me inside? (REUBEN *takes his hand and leads him carefully off.*) (*Blackout.*)

(*At this point, a short invitation or devotion would probably be appropriate. This is, after all, a parable, and some may not understand it unless they are told.*)

A Door of Faith

A Missionary Play in Five Scenes

I wrote this for the Foreign Mission Board of the SBC, as the theme interpretation for daily mission studies at Ridgecrest and Glorieta during Foreign Missions Week in 1974. One ten-minute scene was performed each day. Since then, the play has been done both in sections and as a single performance, lasting just under an hour. There is humor, as Paul and his friends interact with modern conveniences and sound very much like Baptists of today. Its purpose is to help Christians in the present to identify the missionary call and respond to it. The play can be used in many ways—as a single evening's service for special missions emphasis, or as a weeklong "special attraction" to add interest to a revival, a week of prayer, or a GA/RA camp. Since the cast is small and props are few, it can be easily toured and could be a valuable addition to any program where the call of God to a life of service needs to be considered.

Cast of Characters

3 men, 2 women

Pastor

Epaphras

Paul

Lydia

Mother of Epaphras

Setting

The First Church of Antioch
This play is dedicated to Zeb and Evelyn Moss

SCENE I (A Door of Faith—Report)

(*The service begins as it normally would. After the song service,*
PAUL, EPAPHRAS, *and* PASTOR *join the regular church staff
on podium. They are costumed in robes, beards, and sandals,
but act as naturally as if clothed in business suits. At time for
play, a staff member moves to microphone and introduces the*
PASTOR *of the First Church of Antioch. "Won't you come,
please, sir?" Lights dim. Spot up on* PASTOR, *at podium.*)

PASTOR: Thank you, sir. (*Looks behind him at men in suits,
back out again.*) Is that the new style in Rome these days?
Well, I'm sure we'll all be wearing them soon. Now, brothers and sisters of Antioch—ah, is this thing on? (*Snaps
fingers at mike.*) Yes? Good. Brother Paul, we've put this in
since your last visit with us here. It's called a P. A. system.
Oh, but of course, a world traveler, a missionary like yourself would have seen these things before. Are you sure this
is on? Humph. Well. Tonight it's a real joy to welcome back
into our services the apostle Paul. Many of you know him
personally from the years he served with us here in this
church in Antioch. He's just returned from an extended
missionary journey and has come to speak to our hearts
about the need of foreign missions. I know you are excited
as I am to have a real live missionary in our midst, and I'm
sure that later on he'll consent to answer a few questions
about some of the strange peoples he's seen and, ah, maybe
tell us about different animals—for the children, of course.
He'll come in just a minute, after brother Epaphras comes

to lead us in a hymn. Brother Paul, we welcome you. (*He sits;* EPAPHRAS *comes to mike.*)

EPAPHRAS: Let's all stand together and sing hymn number 304 (1975 *Baptist Hymnal;* page 457 in 1956 *Baptist Hymnal*)—"Send the Light." Perhaps we could have a little light to see the words? (*Lights come up.*) Yes, thank you! The first verse only, let us sing! "There's a call . . ." (*Congregation joins in this song.*) Thank you; will you be seated. (EPAPHRAS *sits; lights dim as* PAUL *comes to podium.*)

PAUL: Brother Pastor, thank you. Brother Epaphras, thank you for leading that fine singing. My brothers and sisters of Antioch, it's good to be back with you, to share with you some of our experiences. I'm pleased to see your growth—I assure you, brother Pastor, the size of the congregations I've been addressing lately haven't warranted the use of these new P. A. systems, so no, I hadn't seen one before. Nor have I seen all that many strange animals. What I've seen a lot of lately is faces. Faces of people who have needs, who need Jesus Christ. I wish there was a way I could show you these faces—if I could just . . . just project pictures of them on a wall and let you *see* them, see the needs in their eyes, the idea of missions would become much more real to you. But I guess, really, not even pictures could express what I want to relate to you. Not even pictures could convey to you the joy of love shared in Jesus Christ with a stranger from a strange land. And yet, you *need* somehow to know, for this church is *personally* involved with these people, and they send their thanks to each and every one of you, for being willing to share with them the gospel of Christ! You are involved in world missions, and you need to be aware of what's going on.

What does the word *missions* mean to you? Well, perhaps the pastor has touched on it a little—perhaps you view world missions as traveling to exotic places, meeting people who live very differently from the way you do, seeing animals. . . .

But the thing you need most to know about missions is

that those strange people *are* people. People, just like you and me! Who, for all the fact of their differing languages and customs, have needs that must be ministered to.

What are their needs? Well, tell me, what are your needs? Food? Skills to earn a living? Good health? All these needs that you have, they share with you. But the most pressing need they have is one that has already been met in your lives by the presence of Jesus Christ. It is that spiritual need for a right standing with God, which can only come through hearing and receiving the message of salvation.

But how can people believe in Jesus if they've never heard of him? How can they hear about him without a preacher? And how can men be expected to preach to them unless you send them? You have a marvelous instrument here for making a man's voice heard throughout a great hall. (*Snaps fingers in front of microphone.*) Even my fingers snapping can be heard all over the building. Listen! The Lord has a wonderful instrument for making His voice heard throughout the whole *world* . . . and that instrument is you and me. How can those men in foreign lands hear the gospel of Jesus Christ, if *we* do not serve as the amplifiers of God's message?

This church has a history of being a mission-minded church. Barnabas and I have felt so wonderfully your prayers with us. But it has become apparent that two men, sharing the gospel daily with whomever we meet, cannot hope to meet this basic need of the multitudes who need to hear the gospel. We need *more* to go out. We need more missionaries from *this* church, set apart as Barnabas and I were, to share the gospel with the world at large! We need, most of all, to be responsive to the command of Christ our Lord, when he said, "Go ye therefore, and teach all nations, baptizing them in the name of the Father, and of the Son, and of the Holy Spirit, teaching them to observe all things whatsoever I have commanded you: and, lo, I am with you always, even unto the end of the world."

Let us pray together. Our Father in heaven. We sincerely pray that you would touch the lives of those here today whom you would have serve you on foreign fields. Oh Lord, the needs are so great, and so very real. We know, Lord, that the vast majority of this group you would have to remain here in Antioch, sharing your message with those around them. But we pray that you would touch us all, Lord, with the realization that we are *all* involved in missions. We pray your blessings on this church in Antioch, in the name of your Son, Jesus Christ. Amen. (*As with all monologues, this may be memorized, or* PAUL *can leave notes on the podium and refer to them in a natural way.* PAUL *begins to move away, is stopped by the* PASTOR, *who speaks as if the meeting is over.*)

PASTOR: Oh, brother Paul, thank you for that fine report. I know our people's hearts were stirred. I suppose I had a little of that missionary stereotype in my own mind—the animals and all. Say, you don't happen to have any slides of the places—no, I suppose you wouldn't, would you? Well anyway, I enjoyed that. Oh, looks like I'd better get to the back door before everyone gets out . . . (*Exits down the aisle, shouting.*) Ah, *hello,* Mrs. Epictetus! How was the attendance in the children's department this morning? (*He's off.*)

EPAPHRAS: Brother Paul? (*Takes* PAUL*'s hand.*) I certainly enjoyed that!

PAUL: Thank you, Epaphras, thank you.

EPAPHRAS: I was wondering—is there a time we could get together and talk over some of the specific needs you've seen?

PAUL: Certainly. I'm staying in the pastor's home. Would you care to come along with me and just visit some?

EPAPHRAS: Yes, I—I'd just like to know a few more details.

PAUL: I made this report to the church tonight feeling that the Lord would speak through it to individuals such as yourself. As I said, missions is a very *personal* thing—and the Lord needs persons to do it!

EPAPHRAS: Well, of course, I don't know exactly what the Lord is calling me to do. But I do want to learn more about it. I'll see you in a few minutes, then?

PAUL: That's fine, Epaphras. (EPAPHRAS *exits.* PAUL, *looking after him, sighs.*) Thank you, Lord. (*Blackout.*)

SCENE II (A Door of Faith—Support)

(*Lights up on* PAUL, PASTOR, *and* EPAPHRAS, sitting in easy chairs eating pie and drinking coffee—coffee table, modern chairs, yet still dressed in robes, etc.)

PAUL: Pastor, you tell your wife she makes the *best* apple pie I ever tasted!

PASTOR: She does do mighty fine. Mighty fine. Wait until you taste her fried chicken. Epaphras, can I get you another piece?

EPAPHRAS: No, thank you. . . .

PASTOR: More coffee?

EPAPHRAS: No, please—keep me awake all night! (*Looks at* PAUL.) I may just have some trouble sleeping anyway, after that message this evening.

PAUL: Well, in a way I hope you do, Son. I think we all sleep a little too soundly these days. When I think of the challenge we've been given, I sometimes wonder how any Christian can sit back in his chair and say, "Let George do it."

EPAPHRAS: But what exactly *is* there to do? Take a person like me, for example. I make rugs for a living. What could I do in a foreign land that I couldn't do here in Antioch?

PAUL: The question isn't that so much as it is—Where does God want you to do what you *can* do?

EPAPHRAS: I don't understand.

PAUL: You make rugs? I make tents. Those skills are not very different whether they are practiced here in Antioch, in Jerusalem, across the water in Cyprus, or, I suppose, even in Rome. You could be a rug maker anyplace in the world. But let me ask you: are you a Christian rug maker here in Antioch?

EPAPHRAS: Of course.

PAUL: Do those who work with you know that you are a Christian? In the stall next to yours in the marketplace, do they talk about "Epaphras the Christian?"

PASTOR: I think I could answer that. Epaphras has been one of our most faithful brothers here in Antioch.

PAUL: I praise God to hear it! The question then becomes: Where do you think God wants you to serve? Could it be that he wants you to be, rather than *one* of the Christian rug makers in the marketplace here in Antioch, *the* Christian rug maker in, say, Colossae? I can name you a dozen cities that need someone to come in and go to work, to *live* the Christian life there in the marketplace, to share the Christian message with whoever will listen. There may be nothing you could do in Derbe that you couldn't do here in Antioch. People need to hear about Jesus in both cities. The question is: Where does God want you?

EPAPHRAS: But—if that's the case, what's the difference between the missionary and some church member?

PAUL: None at all, my friend. None at all. You see, crossing the border doesn't make one a missionary, anymore than crossing the street does. Setting someone apart doesn't make one a missionary, either. A missionary is someone with a mission to perform—and we've been given a mission by the Lord to tell the whole world about Jesus Christ!

PASTOR: So you could be a missionary right here in Antioch, Epaphras. . . .

PAUL: You already *are*. (*Pause.*)

EPAPHRAS: But if God wants me some other place—I need to make myself available to be sent there. (*Pause.*) You said you could name a dozen cities that need someone to come?

PAUL: Salamis—Paphos—Attalia—Perga—Lystra—Derbe— Iconium — Hieropolis — Colossae — Smyrna — Ephesus —Rome itself.

EPAPHRAS: I've never *heard* of some of those places!

PAUL: And they've never heard of Jesus. I pray that the Lord will give me the chance to visit those I haven't, but surely He has prepared other men who will be willing to go and stay, to invest their lives in sharing with the people of these cities the world of God! It's such an exciting story; how can we sit and keep it to ourselves?

EPAPHRAS: I . . . I need to pray about this. I have so many questions. You and Barnabas travel together. Who would I go with?

PAUL: I'm sure the Lord will provide you with a partner in your journey, if that is His wish. Epaphras, there are many questions in anything we do. I've found it's easiest just to let God answer them one at a time. You question now whether you should go. Settle that one first.

EPAPHRAS: I need to get home. My wife will be wondering.
    . . .

PAUL: Let's pray before you go. Our Lord, we ask a special blessing on our brother Epaphras as he seeks to know your will for him. Grant him insight, we pray, in Jesus' name. Amen. (*They stand.*)

EPAPHRAS: Brother Pastor, thank you for the pie.

PASTOR: Thank my wife, son. I'm just an eater, myself.

EPAPHRAS: And thank you, Paul. I'll be speaking to you again. Good night!

PAUL: Good night.

PASTOR: 'Night, Epaphras. (EPAPHRAS *exits;* PAUL *and* PASTOR *sit again.*) He's a fine boy.

PAUL: He seems to be. I'm glad I had a chance to talk to him.

PASTOR: Can't see how he'd make it to the mission field, though. His mother is against it—wants to keep him home.

PAUL: The Lord has ways of changing people's minds.

PASTOR: Ah, yes, isn't it the truth! (*Sighs.*) I surely do wish He'd change a few minds around here.

PAUL: You mean . . .

PASTOR: Did you notice the congregation tonight? Divided right down the middle. Jews on one side, Gentiles on the other. Both of us are Jews, Paul, so I feel I can speak frankly to you. I tell you, it's got me down.

PAUL: I can understand.

PASTOR: Of course they'll tell you a half-dozen reasons why, but it all comes down to racial prejudice, and we both know it. That's the last thing they'd admit, though. Some of our brethren have the hardest time seeing people as people.

PAUL: It's the same way everywhere, my friend.

PASTOR: Well somehow, someway, this squabble between Jew and Gentile is going to have to be resolved, or it's going to split this church wide open.

PAUL: It *will* be resolved, Brother Pastor. I haven't told many others yet, but I intend to go on to Jerusalem from here. I want the brethren there to know the wonderful things God has been doing!

PASTOR: Well, watch yourself, or they might try to take your head off. I tell you, we have so *many* problems dividing us up, keeping us from doing what the Lord commissioned us to do. Over here's a group who believe they're the only ones who have the Holy Spirit, and over there's a group that says the Spirit that has hold of this group is anything *but* holy, and then there's this great big group of those who are satisfied to just come to church and sit. Ah, Paul, sometimes it's enough to make me want to pack my bags and become a missionary myself!

PAUL: You think by that you'd get away from the problems?

PASTOR: Oh no, I'm not so naive as to think that. It's just that at times I think even a fresh set of problems would be a relief.

PAUL: At times you do.

PASTOR: That's right.

PAUL: But not always.

PASTOR (*smiles*):   No. And that's why I stay, I suppose. God put me here. He's at work here. And it sure is exciting to watch Him at work!

PAUL: As we said to Epaphras—you *are* a missionary. Right here.

PASTOR: Yes. Still, when I hear about faraway places and peoples, and the needs, I sometimes wish. . . .

PAUL: Just the opposite of what I wish sometimes as I travel. "Just to be home for a while, Lord," I hear myself praying. But when I get home, it seems I'm not there a week before I'm wanting to go again. This is *your* place of service. It's where you belong.

PASTOR: I suppose you're right. But I want to be of some service to the world mission effort.

PAUL: You are! That young man who was here a moment ago—would he have been here if you hadn't supported missions? That's your mission, to stay and build, even as mine is to go. Tell me, if you don't build churches here, who's to support those who go and tell? Undergird the mission program here in Antioch, my friend. Stay here and hassle out these problems. Meet them head-on, with the love of Christ in your heart. And lead this *church* to support missions—in prayers, in finances, and in manpower! Where else are our new missionaries to come from? Relax, my friend, and bloom where God has planted you! (*Blackout.*)

SCENE III (A Door of Faith—Sacrifice)

(EPAPHRAS *is seated at a table in his home, finishing a meal. His* MOTHER *and* LYDIA, *his wife, are moving around him, finishing various chores.* EPAPHRAS *is deep in thought.*)

LYDIA: Can I get you a piece of cake, honey?

EPAPHRAS: Hmm? Oh, no. No, thank you.

MOTHER: You've been awfully quiet today.

EPAPHRAS: Um-humm.

MOTHER: Worried about something?

EPAPHRAS: Hmm? Oh. No. Not really.

MOTHER: Not really?

EPAPHRAS: No. Ah, honey?

LYDIA: Yes?

EPAPHRAS: Would you get me a piece of cake?

LYDIA (*smiling at* MOTHER): Sure. (*Goes to get cake.*)

MOTHER: Not worried, hmm?

EPAPHRAS: No, Mom. Why do you ask?

MOTHER: Oh, no reason.

EPAPHRAS: That looks good, Sweetheart. Thanks. (*Begins to eat cake* LYDIA *has set before him.*)

MOTHER: Well, what is it that you *aren't* worried about that has you so deep in thought?

EPAPHRAS: Humm? Oh, I've just been thinking about what Paul said last night.

MOTHER: I guessed it. And you're thinking you want to go.

EPAPHRAS: I'm not sure I want to go, Mother—that isn't the question. I'm wondering if God is calling me to go.

MOTHER: Son, why would God call a rug maker to go as a missionary? Missionaries are *preachers,* Epaphras, so why don't you just forget it?

EPAPHRAS: That's what I thought, too, until I talked with Paul last night. Did you know he works as a tentmaker to support himself while he tells others about Jesus?

MOTHER: No, I didn't, but I don't see why a man with his education should have to work at something like that!

EPAPHRAS: I get the impression he likes it. It gets him close to the people. I think you have a distorted view of him, Mom. He's not like you think. He's human.

MOTHER: Well, I wonder.

EPAPHRAS: Well, you won't after tonight. I've invited him for dinner.

LYDIA (*surprised*):   Oh, really?

MOTHER: Aren't you glad he told you, Lydia!

LYDIA (*laughing*):   Yes, I think I *am!* You don't think you might have told me sooner, do you?

EPAPHRAS: There's plenty of time. And like I said, he's really just a person. He won't mind what you fix.

MOTHER: Well, perhaps he is, but that isn't any reason for your wanting to run off and be like him! You might sell a Roman soldier a rug and find he's very personable, but you don't start planning to run off and join the Praetorian Guard.

EPAPHRAS: Relax, Mom. I'm not going to "run off" anyplace.

MOTHER: But you're thinking about it!

EPAPHRAS: I'm thinking about what God wants me to do, Mother. That's all.

MOTHER: Well, then tell me, what exactly do you believe He wants you to do?

EPAPHRAS: I'm—I'm not sure yet.

MOTHER: Good, then maybe you'll listen to a little sense, hmm? First of all, what about the business? If you decide to be a missionary and travel off Lord knows where, who's going to run it? Your father spent his whole lifetime building our rug business into what it is today. Would you just throw all that work away?

EPAPHRAS: I'm sure that if the Lord wants me to go elsewhere to share His message, He'll provide a way to care for our financial needs.

MOTHER: You *think* maybe He will.

EPAPHRAS: No, I have *faith* that he will. Paul said I should take this decision one step at a time, anyway. I want to do that, Mom.

MOTHER: But where will you go? Why this wish to travel away from *home* to tell people about Jesus! Why can't you just—just tell our next-door neighbors!

LYDIA: He already did that, Momma. Our next-door neighbors are Christians, remember?

MOTHER: Well—then—our next-to-next-door neighbors! Why go to live with foreigners? They don't know you, and you don't know them. What business is it of ours what they believe?

EPAPHRAS: Mom, now really!

MOTHER: Oh, I'm sorry, but this has me upset!

EPAPHRAS: I believe I knew that. . . .

MOTHER: And what about Lydia? You just want to go off and leave her by herself? And the children? You need to think of these things, Son! I'm not just trying to find excuses to keep you here; these are things you simply must consider!

EPAPHRAS: Mother, I just don't know yet *what* I'm to do! I haven't discussed it with Lydia yet. Honey, it's not that I haven't been thinking of you. I . . . I want to be sure in my own mind first what I need to do—before we try to make any plans. But I already have had to face this fact. There are going to have to be some sacrifices made, if I go.

MOTHER: Then *think* of those sacrifices, Son.

EPAPHRAS: I *have* thought of them! Have *been* thinking of them! Of course there would be the problem of what to do with the business. But I'm convinced that if God wants me to serve Him in another city, for me to stay here against His will would cause far greater problems.

MOTHER: But the family, all our friends. . . .

EPAPHRAS (*sighs*):   Yes, I know. It would be a terrible thing to try to pull up roots and leave this place, with all its many memories. Especially so to travel to a strange place where people with different customs speak in a strange tongue. The festival times will be hard to miss. I know there will be sacrifices, Mom. But I'd rather sacrifice all those things than sacrifice my peace of mind. If God has called me to go, I'd have to sacrifice that *not* to! (*Starts to exit.*)

LYDIA: Where are you going?

EPAPHRAS: Up the hill—I'm just going to pray. (*Kisses her on the cheek.*) I'll be back after a while. (*Exits.*)

MOTHER (*to* LYDIA): Well, why don't you say anything? Your husband's thinking of running off into the wilds, and you say nothing?

LYDIA: What is there to say, Mom? Nothing's been decided yet.

MOTHER: And nothing would *be* decided if you'd just put your foot down!

LYDIA (*smiles*): Oh, I think you know your son better than that.

MOTHER: Ah . . . you're right. He's as stubborn as I am. No . . . more!

LYDIA: He's stubborn, all right. But this is different, Mom. I can tell. He's sincerely seeking the Lord's will for his life, and he's having a difficult time making a decision.

MOTHER: Well, can't you help him a little, at least, by telling him how you feel?

LYDIA: Oh, I could tell him how I feel, but I'm afraid it wouldn't be what you'd like to hear me say.

MOTHER: What? You mean you want him to *go?*

LYDIA: I want him to be what God wants him to be! If that's to be a missionary, I want him to say, "Yes, I'll go!"

MOTHER: But what about yourself? What about the children? Land sakes, has this whole household gone crazy?

LYDIA: No, Mom. Sit down. (MOTHER *does;* LYDIA *sits across from her.*) We all have to be willing to make sacrifices—even those who stay behind. Don't you see, Mom? Jesus sacrificed his life for us, and then told us to take up our cross and follow him! He doesn't ask everyone to carry that cross around the world, but He does call some to that task. If He's called Epaphras, would you really want to stand in his way?

MOTHER: No, I suppose not. But . . . but why me? Why *my* son?

LYDIA: Even those who remain behind make sacrifices, Mom. If Epaphras should find he needs to go, I'll be willing to sacrifice myself, as well.

MOTHER (*sighs—tired voice*):   Whoever thought being a Christian would cost so much?

LYDIA: Well, Mom, you—

MOTHER: Shhh. I *did,* Lydia. When I dedicated that boy to the Lord (*sighs*), I guess I really knew all along. (*Blackout.*)

SCENE IV (A Door of Faith—Partnership)

(*Lights up on* PAUL, LYDIA, MOTHER, *and* EPAPHRAS, *all sitting at the table.*)

MOTHER: Well, Reverend Paul, it's certainly been a pleasure to have you in our home.

PAUL: It's been a pleasure for me to be here. This was a delicious meal! Tell me, which of you two lovely ladies cooked it?

LYDIA: To tell you the truth, we both did.

MOTHER: That's something you don't see very often, but it's true. We've been cooking together so long now we make a pretty good team.

LYDIA: She seems to know what I'm planning to do before I do!

PAUL: Hmmm. Sounds like Barnabas. At times I believe he reads my mind. (*Chuckles.*) At other times I'm sure glad he can't!

EPAPHRAS: Where is Barnabas, anyway?

PAUL: Staying with relatives in another part of the city. I expect to see him at the meeting tonight.

EPAPHRAS: It must be wonderful to have a friend like him to rely on.

PAUL: Yes, it is. We have our differences sometimes, and I'm sorry to say both of us have somewhat violent tempers, but it has been a wonderful experience to work with him. It's exciting to see how the Lord controls our ministry through the Holy Spirit. When I have been given something to say to a group, Barnabas steps back and lets me say it, while when I am without words, he speaks. Of course, Barnabas would be the first to point out that Paul isn't often without words! (*Chuckles.*)

MOTHER: What exciting experiences you must have had together!

PAUL: Yes, the Lord's work is often exciting. There were some experiences that were perhaps *too* exciting, for my tastes (*chuckles*), but God protected us and brought us safely home. Well, if you will excuse me, I think it's getting close to time for me to be at the meeting. Would you good people care to walk there with me? (*Rising.*)

MOTHER: Certainly! (*Rising.*)

EPAPHRAS: I—I believe I'll stay a few minutes.

MOTHER: Oh?

EPAPHRAS: Why don't you two go on together? There's something I'd like to talk over with Lydia.

MOTHER: Oh. (*Realizes he's made a decision, turns to* PAUL *with less enthusiasm than before.*) Well, shall we go? (PAUL *and* MOTHER *exit.*)

LYDIA (*clearing table*): What's this that can't wait until the meeting is over?

EPAPHRAS: Ah—why don't you leave the dishes for a minute and just come sit down?

LYDIA (*smiling*): Is it that earth-shaking? (*Sits.*)

EPAPHRAS: Perhaps—perhaps not. You know that I've been spending a lot of time in prayer. . . .

LYDIA: Yes. . . .

EPAPHRAS: And that I've been wrestling with a decision. . . .

LYDIA: Uh-huh.

EPAPHRAS: Lydia, I don't quite know where to begin. Ever since we became Christians, I've had the feeling that there was something more in store for me—that God had set me aside for some special service he hadn't revealed to me yet. Well, just about the same time, the new baby came, and then business got to be so good. Well, I shoved it all aside for a while. But now, with Paul's return, I . . . I feel like I know, now, what God wants me to be.

LYDIA: And that is?

EPAPHRAS: A missionary. (*She nods, smiles.*) You're not surprised?

LYDIA: Why, no. Was I supposed to be?

EPAPHRAS: Well, yes, at least a little! You're sure you're not?

LYDIA: I'm sure. (*Smiles.*)

EPAPHRAS: Well . . . humph. Then . . . then that's all settled?

LYDAI: I suppose so.

EPAPHRAS: Ah . . . fine. Well. Now I have to deal with some other problems. First of all, the business. . . .

LYDIA: How were you planning to support yourself? Where are you going, anyway?

EPAPHRAS: Colossae!

LYDIA: Colos—?

EPAPHRAS: Yes! It's about four hundred miles from here!

LYDIA: Four hundred miles!

EPAPHRAS: I know that's a long way, but with the modern roads the emperor is putting in, it's much easier to get around these days. At least, that's what a merchant told me this morning!

LYDIA: You didn't answer my question. How are you going to support yourself?

EPAPHRAS: Why, rug making, I suppose.

LYDIA: Then why not just *move* the business?

EPAPHRAS: Hmmm . . . I hadn't thought of that . . . but I could do that! But then, wait. How would you and the rest of the family get by?

LYDIA (*seeming unconcern, begins to clear the table*): You'll figure a way.

EPAPHRAS: Wait, this is a problem!

LYDIA: It is? (*Sits.*) All right.

EPAPHRAS: And there's another problem, too. . . .

LYDIA: Which is . . . ?

EPAPHRAS: Paul and Barnabas traveled together. They went two by two, just as the Lord's disciples down south did when Jesus first sent them out.

LYDIA: Well?

EPAPHRAS: Who am I to go with?

LYDIA (*smiles*): Why, who do you think?

EPAPHRAS: I don't know!

LYDIA (*rises again to clear table*): You'll figure it out.

EPAPHRAS: Lydia! I don't know how you can take all this so lightly! I mean, these are decisions that are going to affect *your* future as well as mine!

LYDIA: See, I knew you'd begin to figure it out.

EPAPHRAS: You know, it sounds like *you* have it figured out already.

LYDIA: Could be. . . .

EPAPHRAS: Well, if you have it all straight in *your* mind, why don't you fill me in! *Who's* going to travel with me as my partner in this mission?

LYDIA (*sighs good-naturedly*):   You live with a man eleven years and he *still* doesn't notice you. (*Stands.*) Who's going to travel with you? Well, tell me, just who has traveled to church with you these many years? Who's worked beside you raising this family? Who's been your partner up till now?

EPAPHRAS (*pause*):   You?

LYDIA: And why *not* me? Is there some reason why your partner on the mission field can't be the same person who has always put up with you?

EPAPHRAS: You mean, you want to go?

LYDIA: Yes, I want to go! I heard Paul speak the other night, too, you know!

EPAPHRAS: Why didn't you say so? (*Smiling.*)

LYDIA: I wanted to be sure, just as you did! I knew that if you found this was God's will for yourself, then we could both be sure that this was *God's* leadership in our lives and not just our own decision. Now I'm sure. And I'm ready to go. What I want to know is why it never crossed your mind to consider *me* as a possible partner?

EPAPHRAS: I guess (*hugs her*)—I guess because I was thinking so hard about the sacrifices, it never crossed my mind that it could be that much fun! You want to go, too! (*Laughs, hugs her again.*)

LYDIA (*after they break apart*):   Now when you get right down to it, it wasn't all that hard to figure out, now was it?

EPAPHRAS (*smiling, draws her close*):   Not at all. (*Lights dimming.*) I love you.

LYDIA (*quietly, flirtatiously*):   I love you pretty well, too. . . . (*Blackout.*)

SCENE V (A Door of Faith—Response)

(*Lights come up on* PAUL *at podium;* EPAPHRAS *and* LYDIA *stand behind him, at their commissioning service.*)

PAUL: Finally, my brethren, I offer you a challenge: the challenge of a world in need of the gospel, of multitudes who don't know the Savior. I challenge you to examine your hearts, as these two have done, and see if the Lord might not be calling you, too, to share the world missionary task. Epaphras and his wife, Lydia, have expressed a desire to be sent out from this body of believers, in acceptance of that challenge. They have accepted the call of God to go and put down roots in a new place and to bloom where they are planted. They go to serve—to stay. I've asked that they share their testimonies with you, that you might be sure of their call, and be aware of your part in it. Epaphras? (EPAPHRAS *steps to the microphone.*)

EPAPHRAS: Ever since I heard the wonderful story of Jesus and of His love for me, I've wanted to share it. I remember the excitement of that bearded fellow from the south, the man Barnabas, when he cornered me in my stall in the marketplace and began to talk. "Do you want to buy a rug?" I asked him. He laughed, stroked his beard, and said, "No thanks, I wear mine on my face. But tell me, have you heard the story of Jesus?" We sat then, and I listened as he told me of the wonderful events that had taken place in Jerusalem, how Jesus had died for me. It moved me to tears, and there on one of my own rugs I asked Jesus to be my Lord. The rest of the day I ignored the passers-by. . . . I didn't sell any rugs, but I learned so much about how to live, about the peace that passes understanding. And then Barnabas told me the wonderful news that there were many others in this city who shared this love of Jesus Christ. I came and joined with this church in worship and praise—I met brother Paul, though I really didn't get a chance to know him before the church set him and Barnabas aside for a special work. Since his return, Paul has told us so much about that work—Lydia and I have spent hours with him discussing the world's needs and what we might do to help. And we come tonight, asking that you as a church set us aside as you did Barnabas and Paul, for the work God has called us to do. We ask your blessings and your prayers. Lydia?

LYDIA (*steps to microphone*):   It is not a common thing for a woman to speak to this assembly, but I thank God for this opportunity to share *my* call. Epaphras has felt the hand of God laid on him to enter a new and special work . . . and I feel God has called me to support him in it. As he has said, we love this church. We'll miss you all—there seems to be no way of escaping *that* burden—but we will always thank God for the way that you have helped us grow in Christian love and fellowship. It's true that we face a mighty challenge—but we have a mighty God! (*They step away from the podium and freeze. The spotlight holds on both of them as all stage lights dim, and* PAUL *moves to a microphone concealed offstage, to join the* PASTOR *in the dark.*)

PASTOR (*at concealed microphone*):   And Paul and Barnabas passed through Pisidia, and Pamphylia, and Perga, and Attalia, and arrived finally in Antioch, where they had first been commended to the grace of God for the task which they had now completed. When they arrived there they called the church together and reported to them how greatly God had blessed them and how he had opened a door of faith to the Gentiles. . . .

PAUL (*at concealed microphone*):   Paul, by the grace of God, to all the Christians at Colossae: You have learned the truth of the gospel, we understand, from Epaphras, who is in the same service as we are. He is a most well beloved minister of Christ and has your well-being very much at heart. (*Spotlight remains fixed on* EPAPHRAS *and* LYDIA, *who remain frozen into position.*)

PASTOR (*at concealed microphone*):   A door of faith has been opened to the Gentiles. . . .

PAUL (*at concealed microphone*):   My dear Philemon, you should know also that Epaphras, who is here in prison with me for the sake of Christ Jesus, sends you his greetings. . . .

PASTOR (*at concealed microphone*):   A door of faith . . .

PAUL (*at concealed microphone*):   Epaphras, who is one of you Colossians and a slave of Christ, sends you his greetings. He works hard for you, even here, for he prays constantly and earnestly for you that you may become mature Christians and may fulfill God's will for you. From my own observation I can tell you . . . he has a real passion for your welfare and for all of the churches in your region.

PASTOR (*at concealed microphone*):   A door of faith has been opened to the Gentiles. Will someone go and share?

PAUL (*at concealed microphone*):   May the grace and peace of the Lord Jesus Christ be with you all . . . remember my chains! (*Blackout.*) (*In black.*) Signed by my own hand—Paul.

The Rainbow on Its Edge

A One-Act Play of Contemporary Setting

Anyone who knows my wife knows that she loves rainbows. She has filled my life with them, made me conscious of them—reminded me of their meaning. This play is different from all the others in the collection in that it's set in the *now*. The characters are modern young people who face modern problems and who are assaulted by so-called "modern" philosophies. An editor friend of mine rejected this play, saying, "I like it, but it seems to be so *specific*..." What he was saying, basically, was that the play wasn't marketable because it comes down too hard on the scientific, humanistic, and romantic views of life. I was sorry he didn't take the play, but I took his comment as a compliment because I firmly believe that there *is* no working philosophy outside of faith.

The play premiered at *Creations* in Tennessee in 1978. It was one of the first plays included in the Church Drama Service. Think young for a moment, and listen—

Cast of Characters

2 women, 2 men

Rebecca, a young engaged woman; a romantic

Rick, the young man engaged to Rebecca; an idealist

Marion, a sincere young student of science; a realist

Mary Jane, a young woman who is an outspoken Christian

115

Setting

A picnic area, after a rain

(*In darkness: There is a low roll of thunder, then the soft patter of rain for a moment; then this fades. Lights up on* REBECCA *and* RICK, *shaking water from an umbrella.* MARY JANE *and* MARION *enter.*)

REBECCA: It looks like it's stopping! Good!

RICK: You think the rain got to our sandwiches?

REBECCA (*looks in picnic basket*):   Put it this way. I hope you like ham on sog.

RICK: That bad, huh?

MARION: Nice going, Mary Jane.

MARY JANE: I didn't know it was going to rain!

MARION: You might have listened to the weather report like you promised.

MARY JANE: But the day started off so pretty—

REBECCA: Look! (*She points to sky.*) It still is!

RICK: Hey, that's nice.

MARION (*looking up*):   So it's a rainbow. What do you expect after a rainstorm—a parade of clowns?

MARY JANE: Come on, Marion, can't you just enjoy something for once?

REBECCA: I'd like to run under it!

RICK: What?

REBECCA: Run under it! I'd like to find its end!

RICK (*to others*):   My mercenary sweetheart wants the pot of gold.

MARY JANE: No wonder! Have you priced wedding dresses lately?

REBECCA: Look at it! It's so beautiful!

MARION: It's just a rainbow—

REBECCA: So beautiful that—that it's almost sad! For there it stretches, from sky to sky, a thousand miles at a leap!

MARION: More like five or six, actually—

REBECCA: Doesn't it make you want to dance and laugh, to run under it and find its end? When I was a little girl I never wished on a star—I wished on rainbows instead!

RICK (*chuckling*):   Why?

REBECCA: Oh, stars are always there—every night, the same stars, doing the same silent stroll through the heavens to a never changing beat. They're always there—why wish on something that's always there? But rainbows—they come unexpectedly—like a rabbit in a meadow—suddenly there and just as suddenly gone. It's sad, isn't it?

RICK: What?

REBECCA: To see them fade away. Just like dreams, that die in the light of morning. . . .

RICK: You're uncommonly lyrical today, my dear.

REBECCA: I guess it's just my mood.

MARION: How can you get so excited over a simple fact of physics? Light passing through prismatic droplets of rain spreads into the colors of the spectrum. I imagine it happens every day, *somewhere* in the world.

REBECCA: And wherever it happens, it's beautiful. Rainbows are memories to be collected, like the first splash in the summer pool, or a snowflake on your tongue.

RICK: *Uncommonly* lyrical. Been reading Shelley lately?

MARION: I know what I'd like on my tongue. A sandwich, water-logged though they may be. (*To* MARY JANE.) If you weren't going to watch the weather, couldn't you at least have tried plastic bags?

MARY JANE: I didn't have any. Here. Oh—you may need to—ah—peel the paper off. . . .

MARION (*asking*):   The napkin's stuck to the . . . ? (*She nods.*) I hope your napkins are biodegradable.

RICK (*pointing up*):   Look—Marion?

MARION (*eating*):   Hmm?

RICK: Aren't the colors always in the same order?

MARION: Mmm-humm. That reflects the length of the light waves. You see red on the opposite side from violet because red light has the longest wavelength in the visible spectrum, and the violet the shortest.

REBECCA: Leave it to Marion to turn a picnic into a lab experiment.

MARION: Well, it is. You can reproduce that effect in the

physics lab anytime with a prism and a light source. Hey, that's what you ought to get Rebecca, Rick. Then any time she wanted to she could wish upon a prism!

RICK: What do you think this is! (RICK *holds up* REBECCA *'s hand, with diamond ring. To* MARY JANE.) Talk about needing a pot of gold!

MARION: A prism would have been cheaper.

REBECCA (*jerks her hand away*):   Marion, you have the soul of a small green worm!

MARION: Thank you. Since you mentioned it, you see where the green band is? Right between the blue and the yellow. And you know what you get when you mix blue paint and yellow paint?

MARY JANE: Green!

MARION (*mocking*):   Good girl!

MARY JANE: I learned that in first grade.

MARION: Oh, really? And it stuck with you this long?

REBECCA: Actually what you get is the color of mud.

MARION: I'll yield to the expert's opinion. (*To* RICK, *shrugging.*) She got a red ribbon in an art show. What can I say?

RICK: That's right, she did. And aren't rainbows one of your favorite subjects?

REBECCA: Oh, for little cards and things, maybe so—rainbows and flowers.

MARY JANE: You paint rainbows? I'd like to see some!

REBECCA: I don't think so—

MARY JANE: Why not? You're not usually shy about showing your paintings—

REBECCA: Marion wouldn't like them. They aren't "scientifically correct."

MARION (*snickering*):   You mean in some you've got the blue and the red together, and the orange next to the green?

REBECCA: Go ahead and laugh. (*He does.*) I have a right to put colors wherever I want to. It's not what an artist sees in the world that she puts onto a canvas—it's what she sees in her mind.

MARION: And some minds are not "scientifically correct."

REBECCA: That's right. Some minds have the ability to see beauty! Maybe that's why I paint rainbows—because they symbolize something of beauty, a beauty that's all too fleeting. They symbolize—a. . . .

MARY JANE: Promise?

REBECCA (*pause; looks at* MARY JANE):   Why did you say that?

MARY JANE (*a bit embarrassed*):   Why? Well, that's the traditional symbolic meaning, isn't it? The symbol of the end of the storm? The promise of no more rain?

RICK: Oh, I remember that story. *Boom*-boom-boom-boom, *Boom*-boom-boom-boom. (*Beating on imaginary drum before him, looks at* MARION. MARION *catches on, joins in.*)

RICK, MARION: *Boom*-boom-boom-boom, *Boom*-boom-boom-boom. (MARION *continues as* RICK *begins.*)

RICK: I, Chief Tail-Burnt-by-Lightning, travel many moons
from land of tribe. I climb great mountain to find rest at
summit and see the gods make war in sky! One god shouts
—thunder rolls across valley! One god shoots—arrow of
light splits tree! One god weeps—tears drop on thirsty land
and thirsty warrior. Then gods make peace, and god of
lightning hangs his war bow in the sky, for all men to see!
Not, however, before he give stinging warrior his name . .
. (*Rubs his backside;* MARION *convulses in giggles and
"drum" is hushed.*)

MARY JANE (*not amused*):   I don't see why that's so funny to
you. I think the idea has a lot of charm. The God of light
and darkness, ruler of primeval chaos, looks down on those
few who have weathered the storm and who watch as the
waters recede. "This is my sign," he says to his children,
"this hunting bow of multi-colored light. I will hang it in the
heavens as a symbol of my promise—that from now till the
earth splits open in doom there is peace between you and
me." Don't you think that's beautiful?

MARION (*pause, shrugs*):   Yeah. If you go for that sort of thing.
(*He goes for a sandwich.*)

MARY JANE: But of course, you don't.

MARION: Why should I? (*Lighting changes from general to
spots on speakers.*)

RICK (*abruptly turns to audience, as others freeze in place*):
Here we are. The classic confrontation of mind-versus-
mind shared over soggy sandwiches. Here, the artist—the
romantic—seeking the thing that drives her soul, in pastels
and paints and memory. Here, the pragmatic scientist—
realistic, quick, cynical. And over there, the confirmed the-
ist—sure of her faith, if a bit unsure of herself. And me. I
have to smile as I listen—as we play this little timeless
game—for that's what it is, you know. A game. Who, me?
Oh, I'm the idealist—the thinker. It always seems I see the

issues with a bit more clarity than the others—but of course, that's understandable. They view the world through the haze of opinions, opinions born of circumstance of birth. Rebecca, here—my fiancée? Her mother's very chic, and also . . . artsy-craftsy, perhaps? Marion—the child of a broken home. No color there. And then poor Mary Jane: she's been dragged to church ever since she was old enough to toddle . . . previously, her parents carried her there. What they sometimes don't seem to see is the powerful social imperative that binds us all together. We'd be lost without one another! But together—scientist, artist, priest, and idealist—we can make man what we want him to be! Never mind the rainbow, we can dance among the stars! (*He freezes;* REBECCA *comes to life—to audience.*)

REBECCA: It's love, there in the rainbow. Can't they see that? Why don't they open their eyes? Love in a multi-colored band! A belt of colors encircling the world, drawing us together by love! Oh, but some are still so blind to it all. Take Marion there. He sees a picture only as paint, a vision as an optical illusion. Give him a ruler big enough, and he would measure the entire universe, scribble the figure on a scrap of paper, and lose it in his wallet. I don't understand why he doesn't open his eyes! Poor Mary Jane. She's always coming up with this God garbage, no matter what we're talking about. Can't she see it's love that guides the planets, and not some comic-book super-hero of a God? And then there's Rick. Oh, I'm working on him, I have hope for him. (*Looks at diamond.*) Someday he'll look into the depths of this stone and see love and no longer dollar bills. Someday. Oh, we're a pair. He's going to right the wrongs of all the world and put everything into orderly little boxes—then I'm going to come along behind him and paint those boxes in colors—every color of the rainbow! (*She freezes, her fingers upstretched to the rainbow, as* MARION *comes to life.*)

MARION: A rainbow is the refraction of "white" light into the colors of the visible spectrum. Light is a mixture of many radiations in wave form. When these waves pass through a prism, such as the natural prism of drops of mist, the light is refracted, or bent. Each wavelength undergoes a different amount of bending, the shorter wavelengths bending the most, veering toward purple, the longer wavelengths bending least, veering toward red. It's a simple physical process, as plain as the nose on your face—which, by the way, is a mass of bone, cartilage, skin, and cells. (*Pause.*) Facts. That's all there is. And if you choose to predicate your life on something other than facts, you'd best prepare yourself for some hard knocks. The real world knows nothing of mercy. Step off of a cliff and you'll splatter on the rocks below. Not pretty, perhaps, but a fact. Want to prattle about the nobility of man? Think of Hitler and Auschwitz, and think again. Want to sing praises to the power of love? Visit a slaughterhouse. I make no bones about it. The world is real. As for rainbows and gods—well, at least I can *see* a rainbow. (*He freezes, as* MARY JANE *comes to life.*)

MARY JANE: As were the days of Noah, so will be the coming of the Son of man. For as in those days before the flood they were eating and drinking, marrying and giving in marriage, until the day when Noah entered the ark . . . so will be the coming of the Son of man. (*All break suddenly back into the scene before, exactly as they left it. Lighting back to general.*)

MARION: Why should I? Why should I believe in such a ridiculous notion as God? I mean, I understand the need of the primitive mind for some system that would encompass a world he didn't understand—I can see Chief Pain-in-the-Tail—

RICK: That's Tail-Burnt-by-Lightning.

MARION: Whatever . . . I can see why *he* would need the idea. But not why a relatively sensible, sometimes thoughtful person like you would continue to believe it. It doesn't make any sense, you know? (*He picks up sandwich, takes a bite. Pause.* MARY JANE *walks right, closes;* REBECCA *follows to put arm around her.* RICK *comes to* MARION *as girls freeze in that position.*)

RICK: That was—a little harsh, wouldn't you say? Isn't she entitled to her own beliefs?

MARION: She can believe whatever she wants to. I just don't want her shoving it down my throat.

RICK: It looked to me like *you* were doing the shoving.

MARION (*eating*): Good sandwich, even if it is wet.

RICK: Don't you ever get tired of this single-minded scientism? Aren't you ever tempted to feel?

MARION: Of course I feel. What do you think I base my life on? I feel just like every other person does. I just feel with my eyes open. I'm not groping blindly in the dark for something that is true; I open my eyes—and trust what they tell me. I run my fingers along the surface of life and believe what they feel is really there.

RICK: I mean inner feelings, emotions—

MARION: I know what you mean, Rick, you needn't patronize me. I'm trying to help you see. My inner feelings are nothing but the simultaneous responses of my nervous system to sensory data. I've learned to filter my feelings, Rick. To run them through the sophisticated computer of my brain *first,* before acting on them. All these "feelings"—this "love," this "faith," this "racial consciousness" you seem so concerned about . . . they all originate in the same place: tiny electrochemical jumps from nerve cell to nerve cell across a thousand synaptic gaps. At that level it's all the same. Stimulus—response.

RICK: I see. And so feelings can't be trusted.

MARION: You can if you want to. I don't. (*Takes another bite.*)

RICK: Every time I talk to you I get an image in my mind of that plastic model kit they sell in hobby shops—the transparent man, with bones and organs visible through his plastic skin—

MARION (*chewing*):   I made one. Sixth grade.

RICK: But is that *all* you see? Just . . . animals? Worse, are we nothing to you but sophisticated machines made of flesh and blood?

MARION: That's what we are, Rick. Sad but true.

RICK: I don't know why I try to talk to you.

MARION: Then don't. Eat. We came for a picnic, not a seminar. (*Another bite.*) Mary Jane, this tunafish is excellent.

RICK: Didn't you ever care about anything? (*Freezes.*)

MARION (*to self, audience*):   Care? Me, care? Whoever cared for me? (*He wanders downstage.*) No one cares. Not really. It's all a lie we tell ourselves and others, to keep life from boring us to death. We eat, we sleep, then wake to eat again, and when we're rested and filled we make up games of care to pass the time to the next meal. (*Softening.*) Besides, it does no good to care. My caring never put a dent in the cycle of life. (*Pause.*) I used to have a rat named Ralph. A pet, you might say—a friend, even. Ralph didn't seem to mind being seen with me. I used him in an eighth-grade science experiment. I was going to test him, to see how fast he learned, and I built a maze for Ralph to run— took me two whole weeks to build it. He did real well the first day—I put him in his cage and went to bed, and tossed and turned, unable to sleep for thinking of the data I had collected. I woke up the next morning—and Ralph was dead. My mother told me to throw him in the trash, but I couldn't do that. I buried him. Did my project on the Mich-elson-Morley experiment instead. (*Pause.*) Strange, though. I remember making a little cross of two twigs, and putting it on Ralph's grave. I don't know why I did it, but I did it. (*Walks back to resume place;* RICK *unfreezes.*) Care? What's there to care about?

RICK (*sighs*):   Maybe you're right. Maybe I should just drown *my* feelings in a ham sandwich.

MARION: Better get one from the bottom of the basket, or the sandwich may drown you. (*They close to audience as* MARY JANE *and* REBECCA *open up.*)

REBECCA: You're not really upset, are you? You know Marion never thinks before he speaks.

MARY JANE: I'm all right. It's just that . . .

REBECCA: What?

MARY JANE: It's just sad, that's all. To be so pent up inside himself that he can't even allow the possibility of God—

REBECCA: Yeah. I guess he just doesn't feel he can let go and love anyone else. He doesn't trust anyone. So he builds a shell to shut out the world, and traps himself inside it.

MARY JANE: I guess so.

REBECCA: There's only one thing that can crack through to a person like Marion.

MARY JANE: And what's that?

REBECCA: Love, of course! He needs to feel needed. We all do—to feel appreciated and valued. You do!

MARY JANE (*smiles, nods*):   Sure I do.

REBECCA: So you've just got to love him out of it.

MARY JANE: You're probably right. That's what Jesus did. He loved people out of themselves.

REBECCA: Yeah, well, wasn't he the one who said love is God?

MARY JANE: I—think that was the other way around—God is love . . .

REBECCA: God is love, love is God, it's the same thing, isn't it?

MARY JANE: Well—

REBECCA: Because what's really important is the love. You know, the relationship, the mutual giving.

MARY JANE: I don't know. I think the most important thing is God—

REBECCA: What difference does it make what you call him? God, Krishna, Allah, they're all just names that stand for the same thing, aren't they?

MARY JANE: I—don't know. But I don't think so.

REBECCA: Well, you're the God expert, so I won't argue with you, but as far as I'm concerned love is the key word in *any* religion. I think if we could just get all the religions to quit arguing with one another and just start loving, this world would be a lot more beautiful.

MARY JANE: Well—

REBECCA: I've got a better idea. Why don't we just start over! Throw away all these old religions and start a new one! Hey, and you know how they've all got their symbols, like with Christians it's a cross and with Jews it's a star of David? Well, we could toss out the old symbols, too, and use a symbol everyone can understand! The rainbow!

MARY JANE: Are you serious?

REBECCA: Well—it's just an idea.

MARY JANE: Of course! That's what you've already done!

REBECCA: What?

MARY JANE: You've already made your own religion—and the rainbow is your symbol!

REBECCA: I don't think I like the way you re saying that.

MARY JANE: There's one problem, Rebecca. None of us can seem to agree just *what* that rainbow symbolizes. To you it may mean love, but to Marion it's just a natural phenomenon.

REBECCA (*pause, then politely*): That's what I was trying to say. He needs to be loved until he can give love. Then he would understand—

MARY JANE: But who's going to do the loving? Are *you* going to?

REBECCA (*slight smile*): I don't think Rick would take to that idea—

MARY JANE: Then who? Who has the power to love the entire world into loveliness? *I* sure don't. If bringing this world together in love depended on *my* supply of love, the world would never survive the day.

REBECCA (*testy*): I thought that was what your Jesus was supposed to do.

MARY JANE: But only by the power of *God*, Rebecca. Not by the power of love.

REBECCA: Oh, you're just not understanding me! I keep trying to communicate with you and you keep sticking this word "God" in my way!

MARY JANE: Well, you keep sticking "love" in mine! Come now, Rebecca, haven't you ever seen how false that word "love" can be? Have you never seen "love's" ugly backside? (*She freezes.*)

REBECCA (*to self, audience*):   Ugly? Love, ugly? How can the most beautiful thing in the world be . . . ugly . . . (*Thoughtfully.*) Of course, the word can be ugly, I guess . . . if misused . . . and . . . it has been misused. (*Sadly.*) In the front seat of a Ford I heard it misused once—I did that damage to it with my own lips. I didn't mean to damage love, only to experience it—to know how that word could feel, spoken intimately in a private place. I . . . called it love . . . it felt like love . . . but it wasn't. Yet we played the word game together without admitting it was that, growing more in love with the sound of love, of love, of love . . . (*Very sadly.*) of love. And that night I shredded the portrait of a butterfly, freshly painted just that afternoon. I still have the pieces, buried in my drawer at home. Ugly? Oh, yes. (MARY JANE *unfreezes.* REBECCA *pastes a plastic smile across her face.*) Ugly? How could love be ugly? Come on, let's eat some sandwiches. We didn't come up here to pry into one another's secrets; we came up here to have fun.

MARY JANE: But don't you see, Rebecca? Love is a lie outside of God!

REBECCA (*brightly*):   Oh, really? (*Mock seriousness.*) Rick, I have a terrible confession to make.

RICK: Oh? What's that?

REBECCA: I've been lying to you about my love.

RICK: What?

REBECCA (*laughs, reaches for a sandwich*): Nothing, just girl talk. Forget it, I was teasing. (*Lifts a sandwich.*) Yuk!

RICK: I think we should have put the umbrella over this instead of us.

REBECCA: You're right! Look at that!

MARION: At least we aren't under siege by ants. The rain gurgled the little fellows right down into their holes.

MARY JANE: That pleases you? Marion, the biologist? I would think you'd enjoy their visit, as a chance to observe some of "nature's splendid creatures."

MARION: I've studied ants before. They're interesting.

RICK: You know, they really are. I used to have an ant farm when I was a kid. It really impressed me how they worked together.

REBECCA: Uh-oh, I've heard this before. Get him a soapbox —he's about to make another speech about cooperation in government.

RICK: No, I'm not, I'm just—well, I think they're interesting that's all. They move through their daily routines with such a sense of purpose—

MARION: You know you'd make a wonderful Communist—

RICK: What?

MARION: Just kidding. I know what party you belong to.

MARY JANE: Who doesn't?

REBECCA: That's what we're going to go into, when Rick graduates from law school. Politics, I mean.

RICK: Not *right* then.

REBECCA: Well, whenever you're established enough. (*To others.*) He wants to be president.

RICK: Not president—just . . . a senator, maybe—

MARION: That's good, Rick. Keep your goals low, within reach.

RICK: Give me a break! I don't apologize for aiming high in life. Mankind would never have accomplished a thing if people hadn't always been aiming for something a little better. We've all got to aim high, or this country will just flounder around getting nowhere!

MARION: You just said mankind is *always* aiming higher.

RICK: That's right.

MARION: Then how come our country is floundering around getting nowhere?

RICK (*growls*): Ahh—I know you don't believe there's a political solution to anything.

MARION: You mean you do?

RICK: I'd better! That's what I intend to do with my life!

MARION: Don't you ever worry that if you get into it, you'll compromise your values just like everyone else? (*All but* RICK *freeze.*)

RICK (*to audience, self*):   Me, compromise? Never. There is only *one* reason why I'm interested in political science, and that is because I want to make this world better! We don't need any more corruption, we need some cooperation! We need to pull together! And to work together we need to . . . to . . . compromise . . . (*Painfully.*) I mean, not your values, but your—(*Stops.*) I don't know. What do you have to compromise but the things you value, exchanging priorities for the common good, without regard to . . . the truth . . . (*Stops.*) I worked in a campaign last fall for a local candidate I really believed in. I really loved that man! He said it all, every bit, all those things we needed to hear, and the people believed him! We got him elected. Then, a few months later, stories began to trickle into the newspaper columns—then came a stream of accusations—and finally a flood of . . . truth. So what. So we're all human, aren't we? Aren't we? (*Stops.*) It's happening again. I had a teacher who told me once, "Scratch a cynic, and you'll find a disillusioned idealist." I . . . I polish my idealism every chance I get, but . . . but there's a patina of cynicism settling over me again, and I can't seem to find an idea that will clean it.

MARY JANE (*suddenly unfreezing*):   Because there's no idea that will work! (*She enters his spot.*)

RICK: What? Wait, you can't do that! This is *my* turn in the spotlight! These are my thoughts!

MARY JANE: There's no idea that will work.

RICK: You're invading my thoughts!

MARY JANE: Because mankind isn't just a social animal, driven by a racial need to succeed! We aren't just the sum of our pooled ideas! Nor are we simply emotional beings, unified under the skin by a single well-spring of love!

REBECCA (*unfreezes*):   Now you're invading *my* thoughts!

MARY JANE: We're more than just ideas, more than just feelings—and far, far more than just flesh!

MARION: Now you're invading *my* thoughts! Who gave you
the right?

REBECCA: Yes, who gave you the right?

RICK: Who gave you the right to interfere with our thoughts?

MARY JANE: God *always* interferes with our thoughts—don't
you see? He's there, probing around the edges of our troubled minds, seeking to *know us.* He seeks to reestablish that
relationship he promised in the rainbow—to care, to love,
to unify mankind!

REBECCA: What does He want of us?

RICK: What does He want?

MARION: What would God want with me?

MARY JANE: To show you Himself. To get behind that cold,
unfeeling stare and warm your heart with the light of His
love. To help you see He *is.*

REBECCA: But I already love the world! What would God
want with me?

MARY JANE: To power your love! To put some force behind
it. To clean the word of hypocrisy and lies and set it to work
in an unlovely world. He would take your eyes off of loving
love, and set them on loving people.

RICK: But I already love people! Mankind is the crown, the
mind of the cosmos. What need has man for a god?

MARY JANE: To guide mankind! To bring it together! To
mold us into a single, moral force. Aware of His presence,

empowered by His love, embued with His Spirit, man truly *is* the crown of creation. Without Him . . . we're lost individuals . . . struggling darkly with chaos, in a world that makes no sense.

RICK: How do you know what you say is truth?

MARION: How do you know you're from God?

REBECCA: What makes you so sure you've got a better answer than the rest of us?

MARION: OK, so there are some problems with my worldview. But what about yours?

REBECCA: Yes, what about yours?

RICK: Don't you ever doubt *your* faith?

MARY JANE: Doubt? My faith? Well, I . . . I mean . . . (*Stops.*) Yes.

REBECCA: There!

RICK: You see?

MARION: All right!

MARY JANE: But I still hold it.

RICK: What?

MARY JANE: And the strangest thing . . . my honest doubt seems to strengthen it. (*Others freeze.*) Yes, I doubt. Two years ago I lost a brother-in-law. And I doubted. You see, he was in seminary at the time. I was at school in another town, and when I called my sister he would get on the line, a friendly voice from far away that encouraged me when I was tired. He was even a part-time pastor in a church somewhere. Surely God must have loved him a lot. (*Stops.*) And then the phone rang late one night, bringing my sister's voice, toneless with shock. "We just lost Dan." Lost him—where? How do you "lose" a person? But I knew, of course. I understood. Dan was dead. And where, I wondered, was God when it happened? (*Pause.*) And I doubted. I echoed the cry of a million believers, "Lord, I believe, but please help my doubt!" And through my grief, He touched me—He reached out and touched me—for the light of the world was refracted through my tears. God broke Himself into the colors of the rainbow of His promise. He opened up a dimension neither body, nor mind, nor feelings could explain—He met my spirit and set it free.

MARION: It was all in your mind!

REBECCA: A psychological trick!

RICK: You just *wanted* to believe!

MARY JANE: I *chose* to believe—and He showed me Himself. I offered Him my doubt—and He took it. And then, as I opened my eyes wide and my tears passed away, He resolved Himself again into the bright, white light of the world. (*Pause.*) I doubt. Still. But I believe still *more.* (*Pause.*) Rebecca, you know how you said rainbows make you want to race to find their end?

REBECCA (*frozen, but speaking*): Yes . . .

MARY JANE: When I was a little girl, I wanted to run *under* the rainbow . . . to see what it looked like on its edge. I wondered if it would be thick, or dark, or paper thin. I know, now, what a rainbow looks like edgewise.

REBECCA: What?

MARY JANE: It looks like light. Because, of course, that's just what it is. Like Marion said, all those beautiful colors are always in light, but we don't ever see them until trouble stirs the heavens. Then the light reveals its nature to us. I think . . . I think God is like that.

RICK: You've invaded our thoughts.

MARION: You've interfered.

REBECCA: We'll have to pretend this never happened.

MARY JANE (*sighs*): It's all right. God is used to mankind pretending revelation never happened. (*All snap back into positions held before* RICK *'s monologue.*)

MARION: Well, that's the last dry sandwich. You want to jump in the jeep and go get a hamburger?

RICK: No, thanks.

REBECCA: Not me, I'm full.

MARY JANE: Me, too.

RICK: Sun's come out. Your rainbow's faded.

REBECCA: I know. It's sad.

MARY JANE: Maybe not.

REBECCA: What? You don't think so?

MARY JANE: No. We're just seeing it now on its edge.

REBECCA (*pause*): What?

MARY JANE: Think about it.

MARION (*pause*): Well, I've got a paper to finish.

REBECCA: Yes, and we've got a date tonight.

RICK: We do? (RICK, REBECCA, *and* MARION *are exiting.*)

REBECCA: *Yes,* we do! You mean you've forgotten?

RICK: Well, no, I just . . . didn't remember. . . .

MARION (*from off*): Mary Jane, come on!

MARY JANE: Coming. (*Looks skyward.*) Thank you, for showing yourself. . . . (*Pause—she exits. Blackout.*)

Sculpture in River Mud

A One-Act Play in Verse

How did Adam and Eve talk to each other? Did Cain and Abel argue in verse? Probably not. But I found that trying to put realistic dialogue into the mouths of our first parents just didn't sound right. This play was first performed in 1969 as a winner of the University of Redlands Prize Play Contest. It's been produced a number of times since then, and I'm always pleased by the response. It's difficult to do a play in verse—as those who've done Shakespeare can attest—but it can also be very rewarding. We tend to look more closely at the *images.*

Part of the value of this play is the incorporation of the Cain and Abel story into the creation and fall accounts. I've seen a lot of plays about Adam and Eve alone, and several about Cain and Abel alone, but doesn't it make sense to view the stories as intimately interlinked, the very real family problems of a very real family? Read the play. See if the final question doesn't need to be asked of each of us, over and over again.

Cast of Characters

3 men, 1 woman

Abel

Adam

Eve

Cain

Setting

A clearing, by a river—*outside* of the Garden

(*At rise we see a bare stage, but for two large rocks up left and up center. The scene is an open clearing by a river—the "river" runs parallel to the proconium, and the apron of the stage is the riverbank. Abel's "meadow" is off up right; Cain's field is off left, as is the waterfall. The mountains are up right and all the way across the back wall. Off right is a forest. In the course of the action, a circle of stones ("fire-pit") is made left of center, downstage of the large sitting rocks. (When the play is performed in a church, the large "rocks" could simply be the pulpit furniture.)*

(ABEL *enters.*)

ABEL: Here, Father. (ADAM *enters.*)

ADAM: The clearing?

ABEL: The clearing—by the stream that surges blue-deep with life. Do you see the hills, Papa? I think God lives there!

ADAM: Red clay—oozing with life! This is good, Son. This is very good.

ABEL: River runs west, then turns north—It comes from the mountains. The mountains are beautiful.

ADAM: Clay of life, red with reason, man-made!

ABEL: Could God see from the hills, Papa? Could he see us working, Watch my brother harvest, smile at the song of my sheep?

ADAM: Of this will *I* build—*I,* master of animals, namer of names, caller of callings! I will build of this red clay!

ABEL: Could God hear from the mountains, Papa? My song of lonely longing, Brother's song of breaking pain, Mother's song of lost remembrance, your song of vaulting pride?

ADAM (*paying no attention*):   And when I build him, he will stand! A monument to *me*—a monument to man!

ABEL: When Mother comes, I'll sing my song. And if the mountains echo back, I'll know that He has heard.

ADAM: The rocks are evil, Son—Go help your mother—she may have fallen.

ABEL: Rocks aren't evil, though they're sharp—Bitter battles in the stream glaze the eye with beauty. Water tumbling down the stream rushes on to lose itself in oceans full of love. Rocks hold it back—that might be wrong, yet but for the rocks there'd be no waterfall! (*Thoughtfully.*) Father? Why is conflict pretty?

ADAM: Conflict is pretty for man makes it so. Man rules on beauty—on abstracts and art—Man rules on evil, and *I* am man!

ABEL: But doesn't God rule on evil? For if He doesn't, How should we even know that it exists?

ADAM (*turning back to the riverbed*):   Red clay for a red heart —(*absently*) Your mother may have fallen.

EVE (*entering*):   I did not fall. I only paused to watch God's reflection in the rippling stream.

ABEL: But God lives in the mountains—

EVE: God lives all around . . .

ADAM: God lives in *me*—*I* am God!

EVE: You call yourself that, but you know it's not true. I saw Him in the stream—It was God.

ADAM: The God you saw in the water there was placed in the water by Man upstream. I dipped my palm in the cool liquid knowledge, and Man ran off in the river.

EVE: Man runs off *like* the river! A never-ending torrent of meaningless words, tumbling over your teeth into seas of space.

ABEL: When you were sent from the garden . . . When God closed the doors and locked the gates. . . .

ADAM: We were not *sent* from the garden, We were but *tricked* from the garden! The fiery sword was a thunderbolt —the garden burned behind us.

ABEL: But of the Angel that locked you out . . .

ADAM: The Angel was danger—The Angel was fear. The garden, green with spring, dripping wet with life-giving rain, suddenly startled by scorching flame, turned red. Bled of life, the blackened land screamed "run." We were not driven from the garden by Angel's tongue! Yet the gate was locked as tight, for the burned-off brush turned cold. Then the Angel was death.

EVE: But what of God!

ADAM: You speak of God? Were the story true, you are the least of them that should speak that name!

EVE: Were the story false I wouldn't need to speak it. We only *named* Him once we'd lost that which once we knew. That we understood Him was enough, those early days.

ADAM: Were the story true, I had the right! *I* am the namer of names!

EVE: Then don't call it a story! Call it the truth! Remember God, Adam, and call on Him!

ADAM (*busy digging his hands into the "mud" of the riverbank*): I tire of stories—I tire of Gods. I will build my *own* God, A sculpture in river mud!

EVE (*bitterly*): A copy of yourself? What is your goal, "father of man"? To take God's perfect creation, and pollute it into your own image?

ADAM: My goal is a stamp—a stamp of self on everything I touch, a stamp of *mine* on everything I see!

EVE: Can you never just look without longing to touch? I gaze at the purple, gauze-covered night—the dotted-swiss curtain that shrouds the sun. I stare at the stars and the stars stare back, and my eyes wash over with wonder. Yet you only see it as some kind of challenge! You'd climb on a ladder to scratch at the sky! And could you but reach it you'd tear it wide open to leave us forever with sun in our eyes! And then, tell me, when would we sleep?

ABEL: Are the mountains yours, too, Father?

ADAM: They're mine to give. And I, in this moment, will give them to you!

ABEL (*excited*): The mountains are mine!

EVE (*to* ABEL): Like the river is yours—yours to behold but not to control. In your father's eyes, possession is the right to destroy. Would you destroy your mountains?

ABEL: Oh, no, Mother! God lives there!

ADAM: Possession is not the right to destroy, Son. Possession is the right to create!

EVE (*to* ADAM):   Could he create a mountain?

ADAM (*standing*):   *I* will create a mountain! My hands will
bend the river!

EVE: Create? Oh yes! Mountains out of molehills. Skyscrapers
of garbage and trash, turning green with slime!

ADAM: Someday you'll wonder, No longer laughing! You'll
watch me reach the moon—in one giant leap!

EVE: And when you arrive there what will you do? Salute
yourself, and erect a monument? Come, son, to gather
stones and wood. We'll build a fire to cook a meal to feed
the great Creator. (*She exits.*)

ABEL: Will you leap to the moon, Father? May I watch?

ADAM (*angry*):   Go help your mother. (ABEL *exits.*) (ADAM
turns, goes back onto his knees.) Red clay, oozing with
life—swimming with liquid life-blood, misdirected! If I can
bend you in a circle, away from the ocean and back on
yourself, will you live? (CAIN *enters.*)

CAIN: Look, the mighty maker, communing with the mud!
Feel secure, Father? If the story is true, you wallow in your
mud!

ADAM: You always come to spoil it all. Making your presence
known by your constant belch of language.

CAIN: Don't like the language? But Father, you made it!

ADAM: Never for *you* did I make it.

CAIN: Never for *me* did you ever make anything! You make
nothing for anyone but yourself.

ADAM: And if I do, what of it? I have the right!

CAIN: You have no right to anything . . . Nor have I. I stood on the edge of a rock-filled field, and said to myself, "Of course. You have no right to fertile soil—No one owes you anything." Nor have *you* the right to an easy peace.

ADAM: I have the right to what I will!

CAIN (*mocking*): Come now, Father. If that were so, then *I* would not be here! For if you are to keep on eating, I must stay alive—and I *will* speak. You are a prisoner of your own choosing. You tell me you willed that?

ADAM: I will you to keep silent!

CAIN: And I will tell you to die! (*Pause.*) And neither will wins out. Is this but another lesson of the story of the fall? Not even God got what he wanted.

ADAM: Don't talk of that story to me! I *will not hear* it!

CAIN: Bothers you, does it? Then you may be sure, Father, *I'll* never let you forget it! You may ignore *its* lesson, but you'll never ignore me.

ADAM: I can. I will! (*Turning away.*) I must build.

CAIN: Another "pillar to the sky," like the one that tumbled last place? Or the "mind's mirror pool" that clouded place before? We move on from your failures, for you cannot bear to look—But what, dear Father, if some day we all run out of world? (*Pause.*) Ignore me if you wish—you have before. I only grow your bread, and feed your family while you play at God. But there will come a time, old man, when your body lies as lifeless as the clay between your toes . . . And who will lay you under? I will, Papa. I will. (*Enter* EVE, ABEL.)

EVE (*lightly*): Must you always flay your Father with words he made himself? (*She and* ABEL, *carrying rocks, begin to build fire-pit.*)

CAIN: Were I to flay him with my own, he wouldn't understand them. Or if he did, he'd claim them for his own—he's made like that.

EVE: God-made . . .

ADAM: Man-made . . .

CAIN: Mistake-made! Like me. Or was I? Was I a mistake, or like the story says, a punishment for Mother?

ABEL: A punishment for *all* of us is how it seems to me!

CAIN: For all of us? Are you including me? If not, please do, my loving little brother. If you think that life itself is not punishment for me, you miss your guess. And if that story's true, then I hate God! For making me—much against my will. (*He starts to exit.*)

ADAM: Where are you going?

CAIN: To lay out a field to plant for food. We all must eat, if only to give us strength to fight. (*Exits.*)

ADAM (*watching him off*): He's a curse—*that* much is true.

EVE (*also watching*): And yet I wonder if God did not *intend* him for a blessing. . . .

ADAM: Why do you *cling* to that story? What is there *in* it that's beautiful to you?

EVE: *All* of it—but the end. Was the end so bad that it burned your memory?

ADAM: All *I* remember is the blackened garden. If God was in the garden, then God burned too.

EVE: Yet in the beginning you *knew* God!

ADAM: In the beginning I knew *me!* There was a day that I was born—I don't remember. There was a day when first I stood on my two feet and looked around—I don't remember. But on one day I stood alone long enough to step outside myself and see that I was *me!* No longer an extension of the ground I walked on, I was *I,* myself! And *I* walked on the ground. And *that* is what I knew, and what I know, and what I shall forever know.

EVE: And when you die?

ADAM: And when I die? I die.

EVE: To what?

ADAM: To everlasting sleep—Or rediscovery.

EVE: No thought of God?

ADAM: God exists in your imagination.

ABEL: Oh, no! God lives in the hills!

ADAM: In the hills?

ABEL: Oh yes! I've seen him!

EVE: You've seen him?

ADAM (*to* EVE): Now see what you've done!

EVE: But no one has seen God, my son—not even in the garden. His shadow in the stream, perhaps, His footprint in the sand—But never face to face. You're sure that you have seen him?

ABEL: Perhaps not seen—and yet, perhaps! Maybe *felt* is better—surely felt! And I cried. He's in the mountains, Mother. Have I been in the mountains before?

EVE: The Garden's in the mountains ... You were once in me . . . And I was in the garden.

ABEL: No, not that way, for this I have *seen!* With my eyes, in a dream, or a dream of a dream—Somewhere back where I can't remember. When I near the memory—I mourn. . . .

ADAM: Enough of this foolishness—I must build! Red clay—man-made into meaning! (*Turns back to work.*)

ABEL: And I cry. Alone, I cry. Up in a meadow, ringed with trees, new grown with flowers. My sheep are there, and a great big rock, and I lay on the rock and watch. I look this way mostly, Mother—down stream, towards Brother's fields and this clearing—because I cannot look at the hills. When I see them, I want to be in them, to leave my sheep and climb them, up, up high, where God walks. He calls me, Mother, yet I can't come, for the sheep might be killed or lost. Why did God give me the sheep, Mother? Why does He make it impossible for me to come to him?

EVE: Perhaps He doesn't need you yet—someday He will. And when He does, He'll call—There'll be no wall to block you then.

ABEL: And I do other things there, Mother, when not crying for the mountains—I sacrifice.

EVE: Sacrifice? Your sheep?

ADAM: Sacrifice! You won't allow us near those creatures,

even when we starve, yet burn them up for love of feelings that the mountains give you?

ABEL: Not the mountains, Father! God!

ADAM: It's a waste! A waste of wool and good lean meat. I forbid you any more to do it.

ABEL: But Father, God wants me to!

ADAM: God doesn't want anything! God doesn't exist! On second thought, He does. *I* am God, and I forbid you sacrificing sheep. You understand?

ABEL: They're not your sheep.

ADAM: Of course they are. When time began, then was I given dominion over all the animals.

EVE (*pointedly*): Given? By whom? And when? (*Pause.*)

ADAM: I don't remember. But it's my right!

EVE: *You* never tamed the sheep—they only come to him!

ADAM: It makes no difference. Even if the sheep are *his,* the boy belongs to me!

ABEL: No! I belong to God! (*Exits up right.*)

ADAM: Come back here! (*To himself.*) Foolish . . .

EVE: Not yet the fool his Father is.

ADAM: It's not enough that both my sons openly rebel against me—now *you* begin again! I must return to work. (*Kneels.*) Red clay, full of life! (*She looks over his shoulder.*)

EVE (*sadly*): Red clay. All you see. I see water—deep and blue, liquid color of a baby's eyes.

ADAM: Babies are a bother.

EVE: No. Babies are a wonder! Oh, to have a baby once again!

ADAM: I haven't time. I'll found a race! I haven't time for making babies.

EVE: Or caring about boys, or training youths, or building men!

ADAM: Building men! I'll break my back to build a man!

EVE: You do nothing to help him! You spend no time with him! No wonder he hates you so!

ADAM: Oh. You're speaking of the child.

EVE: He's no longer a child—understand that. And when he speaks of burying you in river mud, he's not speaking metaphorically!

ADAM: Don't waste my time with talk of him, or talk of what he'll do. Remember he has Man to face . . . And Man is mighty yet. (CAIN *enters.*)

CAIN: Man is mighty, is he? Perhaps you'd like to show me! (*Pause.*)

ADAM (*backing down*): I must work.

CAIN: You call making mud pies work? Work is cutting ditches to water-parched land, battling the blisters that raise upon your hands and cry out "Stop!" Yet you can't stop. The day you stop you start to die, you rest and start to starve. Growing grain is warfare—and it always seems I'm losing. . . .

ADAM: Don't tell *me* of the fight with the land! I kept you alive with it! Slaving at menial work, while my intellect longed for the stars!

CAIN: You fed me up tall enough to hold my own hoe, then left me in the field to support you!

ADAM: I'd worked for you! Couldn't you work for me?

CAIN: But what of *my* intellect? What of my wish to dream dreams, to build monuments!

ADAM: You can have no such wish. You only feel the after-glow of things that *I* have done! *I* am the creator—never forget.

CAIN: Never forget? As if you'd let me. (*He starts off.*) (*Throwing bag down by fire-pit.*) There's meal for your supper. I go to search for hungry soil, hungry to grow, well-watered and green—(*pause*), Though looking at you, I don't know why I bother. (*Exits.*)

ADAM (*staring after him*): He hates me.

EVE: You give him cause.

ADAM: What cause! He only exists because of me! You'd think he'd show some gratitude!

EVE: For causing him to live this life?

ADAM: Yes!

EVE (*pointedly*): If I were you, I wouldn't sleep. (*Starts to exit.*)

ADAM: Where are you going?

EVE: To seek out another son of mine who ran crying to a

meadow. Perhaps I'll see God with him and we can weep together. (*She exits.*)

ADAM: Well, don't weep long! I'll soon be hungry! (*To the "clay."*) They don't understand, clay. Red clay, surging with life, squeezing with life down the river bed—We understand, you and I—We two *know!* A molded heart, red clay circulation through a body of mud. An arm, a leg, toes, fingers, ears . . . eyes—We understand. You're part of me, an extension of myself—and someday, clay-man—someday long after I've breathed the breath of life into your still river-moist lungs, After I've dropped with patient care your blue-water eyes into their sockets—someday when you stand on your feet long enough to step outside yourself and say "I *am*"—When I'm no longer man but clay—You'll thank me then. (ABEL *enters.*)

ABEL: Father?

ADAM: What? Go back to your meadow. Your mother is looking for you.

ABEL: No . . . Papa, I want to be with you!

ADAM: With me? Very well. But stay out of my way.

ABEL: I will. (ADAM *returns to work, molding and patting "clay."*) Tell me the dreams, Father!

ADAM: You want to hear the dreams again?

ABEL: Oh yes! I love to hear them!

ADAM: Better than crying over God, is it? (ABEL *looks away.*) All right. The dreams. The first dream is . . . Man shall pluck a star!

ABEL: Yes! (*Pause—puzzled.*) Yet when you built the tower . . .

ADAM: The tower. What a fool I was! Thinking I could build to space! Rock after giant rock I piled, to make that thing! Then, to have it fall . . . Rocks are evil. I don't want to talk about the tower.

ABEL: Then tell me the next dream!

ADAM: The second dream? If man cannot reach that far out, then he must delve inside!

ABEL: And so?

ADAM: And so I built the "mind's mirror pool," to help me in my vision. Have you ever found a deep blue pool, somewhere in the forest—The green of the reflected trees, faded by the blue of its depth? I have. But I could not stay.

ABEL: Where was it! Where is this pool!

ADAM: It was . . . I can't remember. Yet I remember the pool—I remember the view it gave me of what I was within. So I set out to make my own. A mirror pool to belong to me!

ABEL: And?

ADAM: I dug deep. Broke my fingernails on hidden stones, dug as deeply as I could! Shored the sides up 'gainst the river, down so deep I couldn't see out.

ABEL: That isn't *very* deep. . . .

ADAM: I opened up a ditch from the river—to fill the pool with water—to give it depth. It filled—A little murky, I thought then, but I was certain it would settle. I laid there all that day. The next morning, when I woke, I saw that it had cleared! Yet—somehow it was only a pond—And I could see the bottom. I thought perhaps more time was needed, but then next day when I woke I saw green around the edges! My mirror pool, spoiled by slime! I thought of a way to circulate the water—I cut another trench for the river to come in, and opened up the old way. . . .

ABEL: And what happened?

ADAM: The river changed its course. It took my pool for its own—and now the ditch I dug makes the river's bed.

ABEL (*pause*):   But still you keep on working?

ADAM: I will always keep on working. Until Man stands there, upon the moon, and looks outside himself to see he *is*—I'll keep on working.

ABEL: Father, if God wished us on the moon—couldn't He help us get there?

ADAM (*angrily*):   God! Again! You waste my time. (*Goes back to work.*) Red clay wisdom.

ADAM: What are you making?

ADAM (*bitterly*):   Don't bother me. Go worship God.

ABEL (*hurt*):   I'm sorry. I only wanted to hear . . .

CAIN (*offstage*):   Father! Look what I found! It's fresh meat for dinner and already cooked!

ABEL (*understanding*):   No! (*He charges off right; his lines and Cain's are delivered offstage;* ADAM *stays where he is.*) Give me that! You had no right!

CAIN (*off*):   Get away!

ABEL (*off*):   Give me that! You had no right! It's my lamb.
    . . .

CAIN (*off*): That you killed and roasted, yes! Leave me alone! (ADAM *continues to work, building in speed and intensity.*)

ABEL (*off*): I gave it up to God!

CAIN (*off, sarcastic*): Of *course* you did! You've just been having good fresh meat while we've been eating bread! Now get away!

ABEL (*off*): No! You had no right!

CAIN (*off*): You've made me drop it!

ABEL (*off*): Leave it there!

CAIN (*off*): I'm going to . . . ow! You come back here! (*They ad lib, yelling and calling further away, fading out through* ADAM'*s speech.*)

ADAM: Sons. I have no use for sons! Yelling, screaming, fighting all the time . . . No use at all. For I must build a race! Soon now . . . won't be long before you're finished! It won't be long! And when you stand—that one day when you stand—my job will be completed! Almost done! Almost. . . .

EVE (*running on*): What are you doing sitting there! Your sons are killing each other!

ADAM: The eyes . . . I have to get the eyes. . . . (*He moves down to "river."*)

EVE: They ran past me through the woods! One held a lamb, the other a club! Stop them!

ADAM: Leave me alone! Blue water bubbles! Full for his eyes!

EVE: Someone will die if you don't do something!

ADAM: I *am* doing something! I'm building a man!

EVE: You're. . . .

ADAM: Building a man! Yes! Out of clay! If the story is true, then weren't we all?

EVE: Your sons breathe murder! The forest screams! Don't you understand?

ADAM: I will build a man! (*He scoops hands offstage of apron, pulls up "water."*) Get out of my way!

EVE: No! (*She hits his arms to splash "water" over him, he strikes her to the ground.*)

ADAM (*feverishly*):   Always stopping me! Always blocking me! This one time you cannot stop me!

CAIN (*off*):   I'll kill you!

ADAM (*running to grab more "water," runs back to pour it into sockets*):   Yell all you want! Bellow and roar! I've no need of *you*—No need of anyone! *I* am God, and this clay is *my* Adam! Here are your eyes! (EVE *is sobbing.*)

CAIN (*off*):   I'll *kill* you!!

ADAM (*caught in the craze of his pride*):   Quiet now! The world, be silent! The time has come to raise him up! Man! Clay Man! My *only* son, *I* will raise you up! And you'll control rivers, you'll swim oceans, you'll fill valleys, flatten mountains, reach the moon!!! NOW!! (*He falls to his knees and begins to breath into clay-man's mouth; then all is silent but for his breathing, and* EVE*'s sobs. He stops.*) Come on. (*Begins again.*) Come on! (*Blows harder, longer; then stops.*) (*Quietly.*) He doesn't breathe. He isn't breathing. (EVE *raises her eyes to look at him, stops and stares dumbly at* CAIN *who has entered, carrying* ABEL*'s body.*)

CAIN (*after a long pause*): He's dead.

ADAM: You've *killed* him?

EVE: Get away. (CAIN *has laid the body down—she goes to it.*) (*Pause.*) So quietly you lie—can this be death? This mask of peaceful revelation? How many blade-point stars of nights to come will call to mind these sightless gems your father once named eyes? And in the nightmare dark, how many times will I behold you so? Broken. Sacrificed upon your father's pride and brother's hatred—and mother's silence. No matter, now, to you, for you are gone, and if you see, you see beyond all we do or say—but not with eyes. How is it there? Does God walk? I wonder.

ADAM: Then this is death? Thus must *I* lay?

EVE (*quietly*): That's what the angel said.

ADAM (*shifting blame*): And you, his brother, dare to stand and watch? Tremble, boy, quake in dread! There is your mirror! You ought to squirm in fear!

CAIN: I will not squirm for him or anyone. I am alive.

ADAM: Yet you have killed! And if my arm knows any strength, I'll make you suffer for what you've done!

CAIN: How, Father? Will *you* kill me? Whose fault would *my* death be? Yours, father, so quick to see delight in sweet revenge.

ADAM: Someone must pay!

CAIN: I've paid enough already! How can I pay still more?

ADAM: You haven't paid enough!

CAIN: And what's enough?

ADAM: Your life for his!

EVE: So *you* would say! In all your folly, pride, and hate—so *you* would say!

ADAM: And should he not?

EVE: Another son to lay beneath the clay? (*Pause.*) He's growing cold. . . .

ADAM (*in rage*):   It's *you* who should be lying here—not he!

CAIN: Me . . . or *you*. I wish it were you.

ADAM (*aghast*):   You would kill me?

CAIN: I would.

ADAM: I'll kill you first! (*Struggles with* CAIN, *is thrown down by his stronger son, who stands over him.*)

CAIN: No, not you. Someone may someday—but never you. You've done your part. You made me live—and that's enough.

ADAM: No, not for me! (*Struggles again, is again thrown down by* CAIN, *who then steps away in disgust.*)

CAIN: Sometimes at night I'd lay awake, and listen for a call to tell me why I lived—and no call came. Was this my calling? This, to kill? Am I but another lesson in the never-ending story of the fall? Get up, old man, and try again. I've no fear of losing, with nothing to lose, and no gain by winning—the struggle is all.

EVE: Fools! You think that any answers come to those who only question, and never stop to hear? My son lies lifeless for no one would listen! Would you kill again, over his body?

CAIN: If not today, then tomorrow. If not tomorrow, then the next. I've finally found my calling—I am a man who kills.

EVE: So *you* have chosen. (*Thoughtfully.*) And yet I wonder . . . could it have been otherwise if mother hadn't sinned?

CAIN (*shrugging*):   It may have been. Who knows? I only know I am myself. That's all.

ADAM (*to* EVE):   Do you feel no rage? Have you no angry cries for blood to cool the burn this death has made?

EVE: You think that blood would *cool* it? No, Adam. No rage. And no more tears. We wrote these lines down long ago by living without God. Now we only act them out.

ADAM (*pointing to* CAIN):   What about the boy?

EVE: The boy's a man. And if he never chose before the way that he would go, he's chosen now. (*She looks at* CAIN).

CAIN: I'll go. But Mother, let me tell you this before I do . . . When I had found my brother's drying blood on trembling hands—Before my heartbeat stilled from anger into slower, louder fear—As I beheld the death-mask form and freeze, I thought I saw for just a sprinting instant, mirrored in the blue of his sightless eyes, my living face! And here upon my forehead was an alabaster scar, pallid and gruesome, yet somehow fitting! I saw it—and realized I was whole.

ADAM: I see it not!

CAIN: And yet it's there! I tried to wash it off, and yet it stayed! Mother, listen! You once loved me—I know I've lost that now, yet tell me this: What kind of joke does your God play to cause me to kill, then to mark me with the blame?

EVE: Don't blame the Lord for your own choices, Cain—nor for your mother's sin.

CAIN: My mother's sin?

EVE: And Father's, too—though he would never say it.

ADAM: Don't lay the blame on me!

EVE: If not, then who? Blame is placed where blame is due. And here, as there in the garden, the blame is shared by all—Yes, even shared by this. This broken head, and cooling body, cool now as the river mud, must bear his share of blame. And but for love. . . .

CAIN: And but for love?

EVE: We all should die in payment.

ADAM: *Someone* must pay! (*Glaring at* CAIN.)

CAIN: I've paid enough already! Yet I must pay still more, or when I leave, the full cost will come due. I curse God! Not because he made me—if indeed He did—nor even for the mark I bear, though that is cruel. Perhaps I curse Him most because of whom He marked me for—A brother that I almost loved—and not the Father whom I hate!

ADAM: As I hate you!

CAIN: Yet most of all, I curse Him because he isn't there. No God to turn to—No God to cry to—No God anywhere. Curse you, God! For not existing! Curse you, God! For letting me live! (*He exits.*)

ADAM: I had two sons—Now I have none . . . And yet I have this clay—drying new—Hardening in the sun like a molded pot.

EVE: Look. They sleep beside each other on the bank—One only lived to die, the other never lived at all. Can you hear the silence?

ADAM: Peaceful hush. Like morning's dawn through a mist left over from the storm.

EVE: There should they sleep—together.

ADAM: Both of clay beginning, both to clay return.

EVE: Two sons upon the blood-red clay. Both molded from the mud. Twins, though one had lived, the other twin stillborn, sleeps at his side.

ADAM: I had three sons—now I have none.

EVE: And here beneath the river mud the race will ooze away and Man will die.

ADAM: He cannot die!

EVE: And yet he will. Beneath the dust and rust-red mud— There he belongs.

ADAM: No!

EVE: Then what?

ADAM: Why, Man must live! That's all! If not—then who will bury us?

EVE: Perhaps the wind beneath north-shifting mounds of sand—perhaps the sea beneath curling waves. I cannot care. *Now* I know the true punishment of childbearing. The pain is not in having them: The punishment is losing those you've struggled so to shape.

ADAM: There still is time!

EVE: Time for what? To live, to die, to beat the earth to give us food? Time for memory's flood to wash away any trace of joy? There is no time, but only time to mourn.

ADAM: Yet there *is* time! To quench old memories with ones made new! To raise old sons through one newborn!

EVE: To lose him too?

ADAM: No need to lose! I'll keep these memories fresh! This one I'll guide! This one I'll lead!

EVE: And then in times of *deepest* need you'll turn to sculpture river mud into a stillborn twin.

ADAM: No, not this time. . . .

EVE: And yet again! The anguished cry unheeded!

ADAM: No, not this time! For he will be my pride, my own, my only gift for Man to come!

EVE: No mirror pools? No monuments?

ADAM: Only my son! Nothing shall hinder that son's growth! We'll wrap his body in warm sheepskins to keep him from the winter's cold! We'll walk through meadows, teach him songs, and show him how to plant! I will be his father, and he will be my son, and we'll walk beside the mountains and say "See? God lives up there!"

EVE: You mean that!? Really?

ADAM: I'll tell him the whole story, of the garden and the fall, and watch it grow to fullness in his mind!

EVE: Then you remember!

ADAM: Remember what?

EVE: The garden! The fall! The sin of pride! The suffering! The peaceful walks of innocence! The final run in fear! You *do* remember God! I see it now!

ADAM: God? No. I remember nothing but only scorching flames and walks alone. And yet, it's still a mighty story, and he shall love it well. And then in time the dreams of Man will come to him! He'll dream them all anew! He'll find a way to see inside, He'll find a way to climb! He'll ford the waters, forge the sword, write poetry in rhyme! And then when he has done them all, and done them all too soon, He'll reach the moon! (ADAM *is gazing up.*)

EVE (*sadly*):   Oh, Adam. Father of Man. How many lessons before you learn?

(*Actors freeze—slow fade to black.*)

With Bonds of Love

A One-Act Play About Hosea and Gomer

This is one of the most performed of my plays, and it is always interesting to hear the responses of those who see it. Many say simply that they had never actually looked upon Hosea and his wife Gomer as real people before. Others say they feel like they understand this particular book of the Bible better as a result of seeing it "live." But what brings the most joy to me as an author is when the final image, the auction scene when Hosea reclaims Gomer, grabs someone as it first grabbed me, and shakes them into a new understanding of the meaning of Christ's sacrificial death. When the play is done well, it can have a wrenching impact—and I've seen it move those who were under conviction to respond at last to the call of God in their lives. I've preached it as a sermon and done it as a play—the play speaks better.

Characters

1 woman, 2 men

Gomer

Hosea

Narrator (who plays other short parts also)

(*At curtain's rise we see a bare stage except for one square block up center.* NARRATOR *stands center, holding Bible, while*

165

HOSEA and GOMER stand relaxed but motionless downstage
right and downstage left.)

NARRATOR (reading): "The word of the Lord that came unto
   Hosea." So begins this little book sandwiched into the Bible
   between Daniel and Joel. Is that strange to you, that the
   "word of the Lord" should come to a man? An uncommon
   occurrence? Uncommon indeed is the story of this man.
   His very life was a picture of the plight of a forsaken God.
   His message was uncommon too, for, in a time when the
   prophets spoke only of vengeance, Hosea added a new
   word—and the word was love. This is the story of a man
   who loved, whose passion and pain illustrated to the world
   the glory of God's forgiving grace. _____ will play this
   man Hosea; _____ _____ will play Gomer, his sinful
   wife, and I, _____ _____, am your narrator. Since
   there are only three of us, with the help of your good
   imaginations I will be playing many different roles. You,
   too, will be playing different roles. You stand now in the
   marketplace of Samaria, capital of the Northern Kingdom
   of Israel. Jeroboam II is on the throne, and it's a time of
   plenty. People throng the streets; and merchants cry out,
   hawking their wares. You are the people of whom Amos
   said, "They sold the righteous for silver, and the poor for
   a pair of shoes" (2:6). Everywhere you look, people have
   something to sell—goods from other lands, homemade
   merchandise—some sell only themselves. I am a fish vendor! (He turns his back and moves upstage behind the
   block. When he turns back to the audience, he is in the
   character of a fish merchant. HOSEA and GOMER exit
   right and left; HOSEA reenters immediately.) Fish! Get
   your fresh fish here! (HOSEA crosses left to block.) Caught
   this morning in the Sea of Chinnereth! Get your . . .

HOSEA: Caught this morning! It's nearly forty miles to Gali-
   lee!

NARRATOR: What? (Quieter.) Get lost, friend. Don't make
   trouble.

HOSEA: I'll bet those fish are three days old. They're beginning to smell!

NARRATOR: Fish *always* smell. If you don't want 'em, don't buy 'em. (*To an invisible passerby.*) Get your fresh fish here!

HOSEA (*to same individual*): They're not fresh! Don't buy them.

NARRATOR (*angry now*): Come on now, leave me alone! How do you expect me to make an honest living with you standing there chasing away my business?

HOSEA: Honest! You cheat everyone you sell to.

NARRATOR: What do you mean, cheat?

HOSEA: They think they're buying fresh fish, when really these fish are at least three days old. (*Sniffs.*) And starting to rot!

NARRATOR: You think my customers don't know that? Nobody gets cheated. They know what they're paying for, and I know what it's worth. It's good for the economy, see?

HOSEA: That doesn't make it honest.

NARRATOR: Fine. OK. It's dishonest. Now would you get out of my way and let me sell my fish? (HOSEA *stands rooted.*) Look, they got laws against guys like you!

HOSEA: Laws don't make a thing right.

NARRATOR: No, but they sure do make it legal. You want me to call a cop?

HOSEA (*pausing*): I'll move.

NARRATOR: That's better. Fish for sale! Fresh fish! (GOMER *enters left.*) Hey, Gomer, you want fish today?

GOMER: I'm broke.

NARRATOR: With all the business you do over at the Baal shrine? What's the matter? Priests keep it all?

GOMER: Every shekel.

HOSEA: You ought to serve God rather than Baal.

GOMER (*pausing, then speaking to* NARRATOR): Who's he?

NARRATOR: I don't know, but I sure wish he'd leave.

GOMER (*going to* HOSEA): Good morning, sir! How are you this beautiful day?

HOSEA: Disgusted by this filthy city.

GOMER: Filthy! Why, it's beautiful! Just look around at all the fine shops, the many-colored rugs, the lace, the jewelry . . .

HOSEA: And all of it built on lies and cheating. Every merchant is a thief!

NARRATOR: Hey! Watch that!

GOMER: You sound like that weird prophet from the south.

HOSEA: Amos? Yes. I was at Bethel when he came and preached. His message stirred my heart!

NARRATOR: I think it stirred your mind. You're crazy.

HOSEA: And you're bent on destruction!

NARRATOR (*frightened*): I thought I told you to leave me alone!

GOMER: Calm down, mister! (*With a professional smile.*) What you need is a friend. (*She moves in closer to him.*)

HOSEA: A . . . a friend?

GOMER: Someone to share your troubles with . . . someone who'll listen. Someone who knows all the ways of setting troubled minds free. You need a woman.

HOSEA: I have no need of a wife . . .

GOMER: Who said anything about a wife? Who needs a wife when I'm here? Come with me . . .

HOSEA (*weakly*): No . . .

GOMER: We'll go to the Baal shrine together . . .

HOSEA (*jerking away*): You filthy harlot! Get away!

GOMER: What!

NARRATOR: You be careful what you say to her!

HOSEA: You and your kind are leading Israel to destruction! You promise warmth and love for a few pieces of silver! And what do you give? The heat of the flesh, a few muttered lies in the dark, and a drugged sleep!

NARRATOR: It's a good profession!

HOSEA: It's an abomination in the sight of the Lord!

GOMER (*bursting out*): Go preach to the pigs! They deserve you!

NARRATOR: Yeah! Go preach to the pigs! You're bad for business!

GOMER: Get out of here!

NARRATOR: Go on!

GOMER: Leave! (HOSEA *is driven off left.*) Pig!

NARRATOR: He's a strange one.

GOMER: Who does he think he is, calling me names like that?

NARRATOR: Don't worry about it. A guy like that—well, he just don't deserve you.

GOMER: Yeah . . . (*She starts to cry.*)

NARRATOR: Ah, Gomer. Shake it off. The guy's a nut.

GOMER: Is that any reason to call a girl a name like that?

NARRATOR: Well, of course not! Anyone with eyes could tell you was clean.

GOMER (*sniffing*):   Clean? What are you talking about?

NARRATOR (*puzzled*):   Uh—wasn't that what you were crying about? 'Cause he said you wasn't clean?

GOMER (*angrily*):   No! He called me a harlot!

NARRATOR (*quietly*):   Oh. Yeah.

GOMER: What's the matter with you?

NARRATOR: Well, isn't it . . . you know . . . true?

GOMER: I am *not* a harlot! I'm a temple girl—a priestess! There's a difference.

NARRATOR: All right. I'm sorry.

GOMER: That's better.

NARRATOR: You—ah—you want some fish?

GOMER: I told you. I'm broke.

NARRATOR: Yeah, yeah, I know—I meant if you want some you can just take it . . .

GOMER (*bitterly*): In exchange for my "services"?

NARRATOR: No! (*Sighs.*) Can't I say anything right around you? Here. Have some fish. You look hungry.

GOMER: No, thank you. (*Proudly.*) My boyfriends take care of me quite well.

NARRATOR: Your—boyfriends?

GOMER (*pausing*): All right. So the guy was right about me. So what?

NARRATOR: The priests—do they allow it?

GOMER: Of course not. I do it behind their backs.

NARRATOR: What if they caught you?

GOMER: They'd probably sell me on the slave block.

NARRATOR: Oh.

GOMER: But that's life.

NARRATOR: Yeah.

GOMER: I'll see you later.

NARRATOR: Where are you going?

GOMER: Down to the palace. The guards are always good for a laugh. (*She exits right.*)

NARRATOR: Hey, don't forget your fish! (*Follows her off.*)

HOSEA (*has entered on her line; is now kneeling downstage left*): Lord, help me! Help me to help my people! There was a time when you would step down into the world and change it with a sweep of your mighty hand. You destroyed the Egyptians and stopped the Red Sea. You parted the Jordan and tumbled Jericho. But Lord—where are you now? Israel mires herself deeper and deeper in sin, yet you do nothing.

NARRATOR (*has entered upstage right and speaks as God now*): Nothing, Hosea?

HOSEA (*spinning around*): Who's there?

NARRATOR: I am, Hosea.

HOSEA: But who are you? And why are you in my house?

NARRATOR: I am, if you wish, a messenger—God's messenger.

HOSEA (*fearfully*): What do you mean, "if I wish"? If you're an angel, just say so!

NARRATOR: If it pleases you to think of me as an angel, then I am an angel. I was the one who wrestled with Jacob—but I'm also the one who appeared to Gideon as he threshed wheat in his father's winepress. Mine was the still, small voice that spoke to Samuel in the night when he was just a child. It was I who spoke to Moses from the burning bush and who was later to bury him.

HOSEA: Are you—God, then?

NARRATOR: I am who I am, Hosea.

HOSEA (*turning away*): I can't look at you!

NARRATOR: For fear you will die? You will not die. I have need of you.

HOSEA: But won't it blind me to look at your face?

NARRATOR: I need your eyes as well. Come, follow me.

HOSEA: As you wish, my Lord.

NARRATOR: We'll go to the top of the highest mountain— here, where you can see my beloved Israel, stretched out across the land I gave her. Israel! How can I give you up? How can I allow you to be destroyed? Yet I must. For you have played the harlot, chasing after other gods. You must be punished!

HOSEA: You're going to destroy Israel?

NARRATOR: I am. I wanted to forgive her, but her sins were far too great. No one can live in Samaria without becoming a liar and a thief.

HOSEA: But surely there are some who do good!

NARRATOR: No. Her people never seem to understand that I am watching them. Their sins give them away. I see all of them. And the king is pleased! The princes laugh at their lies!

HOSEA: But—to destroy your own people! How can you?

NARRATOR: How can I not? It was I who rescued Israel out of Egypt. Yet now my people sacrifice to Baal and burn incense to idols! I led them with cords of compassion. I bound them to me with bonds of love, but still they turned from me! Now war will swirl through their cities. My people have deserted me. Therefore, I sentence them to slavery, and *no* one will set them free! O, Israel! (*Softer.*) My heart cries out within me—how I long to help you.

HOSEA: God, how can you do it? Your own city, your own people!

NARRATOR: They are no longer my people, and I am no longer their God.

HOSEA: But if you mean to destroy Israel completely, what use have you of me?

NARRATOR: I have chosen you to be an example. Just as Israel has turned away from me, so will your wife turn from you. Then you will carry my message to Israel, who, like an adulterous wife, has strayed from her husband.

HOSEA: But . . . how is this to happen? I have no wife, and I love no one!

NARRATOR: You will meet a woman in the marketplace in the company of a palace guard. She is a harlot, but she will be your wife.

HOSEA: Lord! A harlot? How am I to love her?

NARRATOR: Love is powerful enough to trap you of its own accord—or you will trap yourself.

HOSEA: Then I'll really love her? The very idea is disgusting to me!

NARRATOR: Then you begin to understand my feeling for Israel. Go now. Find the woman—and love her. When you've discovered what love is, and when you've felt the pain that comes when one you love denies you, the words I have given you will take on new meaning. You'll see why I must destroy my Israel. (*Exits right.*)

HOSEA (*coming down to audience; as he speaks,* NARRATOR *and* GOMER *enter from right and walk arm in arm to downstage center.* HOSEA *speaks to himself*): Why me? Why does it have to be me? (*He sits on down right edge of platform.*)

GOMER (*flirting*): Well, it's very nice of you, Captain, to invite me out here away from the others, but I'm sure it must be for some other reason than just to tell me I have beautiful hair.

NARRATOR (*as soldier*): Well, it, uh, it is! I mean, there *is* another reason. I mean, besides that, I mean.

GOMER: Just what is it you *do* mean, Captain?

NARRATOR: Uh, actually I'm not a captain—I'm, uh, just, sort of, well, a corporal, ma'am, but—

GOMER: A corporal! Now you're just being modest. A big tough man like you? You can't fool me. You're at least a captain—maybe even a general! Are you a general?

NARRATOR: Ah, well (*chuckling*), no (*chuckling*), I'm, really I'm only just a—a corporal really.

GOMER (*mockingly*): Are you really just a corporal? Just a corporal *really?*

NARRATOR: That's right, ma'am, I'm just—

GOMER: And what would my little corporal want with little old me, hmm?

NARRATOR: Well—it's, ah, kind of embarrassing—

GOMER (*seeing* HOSEA):   Corporal! Arrest that man!

NARRATOR (*puzzled*):   What? What for?

GOMER: You want to know what he called me? (*She whispers.*)

NARRATOR: No!

GOMER: You can even ask the fish vendor in the market! That's exactly what he said!

NARRATOR: Well, he won't get away with that! (*Starts right.*)

HOSEA (*not seeing him*):   Why does it have to be me?

NARRATOR (*grabbing* HOSEA *from behind*):   Hey, you. Stand up!

HOSEA: What's the matter? What have I done?

NARRATOR: You see this lady?

HOSEA: Of course I see her; why—

NARRATOR: You recognize her? Huh? Do you?

HOSEA: Yes, I do—

NARRATOR: Speak up; I can't hear you!

HOSEA: Yes, I do!

NARRATOR: Who is she? Well?

HOSEA: She's just a harlot from the (*suddenly understanding*)—Oh, no!

NARRATOR: Yeah, you better say "Oh, no!" And you better apologize real quick!

HOSEA: No, you don't understand. That's not what I—

NARRATOR: You denying you said it?

HOSEA: No, it's just that—

NARRATOR: Then apologize to the lady before I knock your teeth out!

HOSEA: Soldier, you don't understand!

NARRATOR: I don't understand, huh? Well, then, come on, you explain it to me. What don't I understand?

HOSEA: This woman is—my wife . . . (*Dazed.*)

NARRATOR: What?

GOMER (*shocked*): What did he say?

NARRATOR (*taken aback*): She's your wife?

HOSEA: I . . . I guess so . . .

GOMER: He's mad!

HOSEA: Listen, Gomer, I don't understand either . . .

NARRATOR: Gomer? Is that your name?

GOMER: Yes, but what has that to do . . .

NARRATOR: How does he know your name?

GOMER: I don't know. He could have picked it up anywhere
. . .

NARRATOR: Yeah, like I could have picked *you* up anywhere!

GOMER: What?

NARRATOR: I oughta run you both in! *You* for procuring on
the street and *you* for letting her!

GOMER: You mean you believe him?

NARRATOR: Listen, lady. Do you know the penalty for adultery in this city?

GOMER: Soldier, you're making a mistake!

NARRATOR: Legally your husband has the right to strip you
naked and throw you into the marketplace.

GOMER: He's not my husband!

NARRATOR: Shut up! The full penalty of the law is to be
stoned to death outside the walls of the city. Is that your
pleasure, mister?

HOSEA: No, really, let me explain—

NARRATOR: All right. Then listen, sister. You've embarrassed me, and I don't forget that. If I catch you fooling
around again, I'm going to see you punished.

GOMER: But—

NARRATOR: Since there's a labor shortage in this city, I'll be
practical. If I find you hanging around the barracks again,
that's it. I'll have you sold on the slave block by noon the

next day. (*To* HOSEA.) You keep that in mind, mister. (*Exits left.*)

GOMER (*seething*): What in the name of all the gods possessed you to do *that?*

HOSEA: The name of—the Lord.

GOMER (*pausing*): You're crazy!

HOSEA: Yes, I suppose I am.

GOMER: Why did you claim me as your *wife?*

HOSEA: You—you are my wife—given to me by God.

GOMER (*pausing a long time*): That's ridiculous. Isn't that a little ridiculous? Your God, who's always so down on adultery and prostitution, giving *me* to you as your wife?

HOSEA (*shaking head*): I didn't understand either.

GOMER: You mean you're serious?

HOSEA: Yes.

GOMER: You *want* me to be your wife?

HOSEA (*looking at her*): Yes.

GOMER (*pausing*): No! Absolutely not. What do you think I am, huh? (*She sits, head in hands.*) Don't you realize what you've done to me? I mean . . . what am I going to do now? I get caught and I get sold as a slave! That's pretty rough; you've got to admit that's pretty rough.

HOSEA: Yes . . . yes, it is.

GOMER: But you weren't thinking about *me*. Oh, no, you were thinking about your God!

HOSEA: Yes . . . that's true.

GOMER: And then you think I'd marry you?

HOSEA (*pausing*): What else can you do?

GOMER: What?

HOSEA: You can't practice your—trade anymore. Where else can you go?

GOMER: Right. (*Head in hands.*) What a mess.

HOSEA: Please . . . please don't cry . . .

GOMER: What else *can* I do?

HOSEA: Look . . . wait . . . look at me. Come home with me. Be my wife. I'll take care of you.

GOMER: I can't do that.

HOSEA: Why not?

GOMER: I'd make a lousy wife.

HOSEA: That doesn't make any difference.

GOMER (*pausing, looking at him*): You really want me to?

HOSEA: Yes. I've been trying to tell you so.

GOMER: I can't cook.

HOSEA: Oh! (*He sits.*) There are a lot of things to worry about worse than that.

GOMER (*getting up, drying eyes—walking away*): This is dumb.

HOSEA: I agree.

GOMER: But . . . I don't love you!

HOSEA: I know. I don't care.

GOMER: You don't?

HOSEA: No.

GOMER: You still want to marry me?

HOSEA: Yes.

GOMER (*pausing*): OK. (*She brushes the hair out of her eyes and looks down.*)

HOSEA: You mean it?

GOMER (*nodding*): Yeah. Well, what else can I do? And if you *want* to marry me . . . No one's ever said that to me before.

HOSEA: Never?

GOMER: Never. I . . . I kind of like it. (*She giggles to herself; he laughs.*) Oh, one thing.

HOSEA: What?

GOMER: What's your name?

HOSEA: Hosea.

GOMER: Oh. (*She smiles.*) I like it.

HOSEA: Thanks.

GOMER: I'm Gomer.

HOSEA: I know.

GOMER: Yeah . . . I guess you do. (*She looks at him and shrugs.*) Well . . . let's go home.

HOSEA (*nodding*):   OK. (*He smiles; she smiles back. They exit right.*)

(NARRATOR *comes to audience from left.*)

NARRATOR: Hosea couldn't believe that he would truly fall in love with Gomer . . . but he did. Once *in* love, he couldn't conceive of ever falling out. He loved her more deeply than he loved himself and greeted each morning with surprised joy that love had at last captured him. Gomer, too, felt these bonds of love; and though there were times she wished she could break free and be as she was before, there were good times, too—times of comfort she'd never before enjoyed, and feelings of peace and security that were bits of heaven to her. At last she had someone to cling to. Hosea and Gomer loved each other, and by the end of the first year she had borne him a son. (*He turns and moves upstage right; he is God now. HOSEA enters past him from upstage right to downstage center, pantomimes carrying a basket, sets it down, pantomimes hanging diapers on an imaginary line.*) Hosea? Hosea?

HOSEA: Right here, Lord! You'll have to excuse me . . . I'm hanging out diapers.

NARRATOR: For your new son.

HOSEA (*smiling*):   Yes, Lord. Have you seen him?

NARRATOR (*smiling*):   I made him, Hosea.

HOSEA: Oh . . . yes . . .

NARRATOR: Call his name Jezreel, for yet a little while, and I will avenge the blood of Jezreel upon the house of Jehu and destroy the kingdom of Israel.

HOSEA: I . . . I *would,* Lord; but you see, Gomer already named him. Joshua she named him. I really . . .

NARRATOR: Call his name Jezreel.

HOSEA: Why? What's wrong with Joshua? It's a good name . . . a leader's name!

NARRATOR: Another baby will be born to lead his people . . . that time has not yet come. This baby will be Jezreel.

HOSEA: Well, all right . . . have it your way. Gomer will be upset, but . . . well, it won't be the first time.

NARRATOR: Do you love her, Hosea?

HOSEA: Oh, Lord, you know I do! She's made me . . . I mean, you've made me the happiest man in the world. And that baby. Oh, if you could know the joy, that great feeling of joy that comes when you hold the son you've helped create in your arms . . .

NARRATOR: I've had sons. Many of them, Hosea. Adam, Abraham, Jacob—and you. Hosea, can you imagine losing that son?

HOSEA: Oh—no. It would kill me.

NARRATOR: That's the price your God must pay to bring his people back to him.

HOSEA: I don't understand . . .

NARRATOR: You needn't understand, Hosea. That time hasn't come. But do understand this. Your joy will fade like morning mist when your wife turns her back on you. Call the boy Jezreel. (*Starts to exit right.*)

HOSEA: She wouldn't do that to me, Lord! She loves me!

NARRATOR: Call him Jezreel, for I will punish Israel's adulteries. (*Exits upstage right.*)

HOSEA (*to himself*):   She wouldn't. (*Loudly.*) Gomer?

GOMER (*off right*):   I'm in the house, love!

HOSEA: Come on out here! I want to talk to you!

GOMER: Have you finished hanging those clothes up yet? (*Enters.*) Why, you haven't even started!

HOSEA: Gomer . . .

GOMER: Yes?

HOSEA: What do you do in the afternoons when I'm in the city?

GOMER: What do you think I do? I take care of Joshua. You don't think babies take care of themselves, do you?

HOSEA: No . . . never mind.

GOMER: Never mind what?

HOSEA: Just forget it.

GOMER: What are you talking about?

HOSEA: Nothing; just forget I ever said it!

GOMER (*staring at him, speaking slowly*):   All right. You're sure nothing's bothering you?

HOSEA: Yes, I'm sure.

GOMER: OK, OK. (*Pauses.*) By the way, I think you ought to start paying the houseboy more.

HOSEA: Why?

GOMER: Because he helps me a lot with Joshua! What's gotten into you!

HOSEA: Nothing, I said. And listen. His name's not Joshua anymore. From now on, we call the baby Jezreel.

GOMER: Jezreel? But we had . . .

HOSEA: That's his name.

GOMER: But we were going to . . .

HOSEA: I don't want any argument now. His name is Jezreel!

GOMER: No! I demand to know why!

HOSEA: There *is* a reason . . .

GOMER: Then tell it to *me!*

HOSEA: I don't have to give you a reason for everything I do! His name is Jezreel—we'll leave it at that.

GOMER (*through her teeth*): His *name* is Joshua!

HOSEA: I'm going downtown. Don't wait up for me. (*He starts downstage.*)

GOMER (*sarcastically*): Got to go save more young girls from a "fate worse than death"?

HOSEA (*angrily*): If that's what God commands, yes!

GOMER: God, hah! Your pious imagination!

HOSEA: I've warned you about that!

GOMER: Go to town . . . I have a baby to feed. (*She starts off.*)

HOSEA: And don't let that houseboy anywhere near you!

GOMER (*stopping, whirling*): What do you mean!

HOSEA: You *know* what I mean! (*He turns, exits off platform and upstage left aisle through the house.*)

(GOMER *stands and watches him;* NARRATOR *enters upstage right.*)

NARRATOR (*as houseboy*): Is he gone?

GOMER: Yes. Did you listen?

NARRATOR: Some.

GOMER: You shouldn't have.

NARRATOR: What was it my master said about me?

GOMER: He told me not to let you near me. (*Turning to look at him.*) Have you done anything that would make him suspicious?

NARRATOR: No, nothing—I've been very careful.

GOMER (*knowingly*): Yes, I daresay you have.

NARRATOR: Well, isn't that the way you wanted me to be? Careful not to let him know?

GOMER (*pausing*): Are you afraid of him?

NARRATOR (*he is*): No. Not at all!

GOMER: You are. And you should be.

NARRATOR: I told you I'm not!

GOMER: Ah, but you are. (*Putting her hand on his lips to stop his protest.*) Am I worth that much to you? Your job? Your future? By law you could be killed. You'd risk that for me?

NARRATOR: Oh, yes. Why, I didn't have anything to live for. (*She laughs.*) I didn't! (*Angrily.*) Why are you laughing?

GOMER (*putting her arms around him*): Promise me one thing, will you?

NARRATOR (*frightened*): Not here! The neighbors . . .

GOMER: Hang the neighbors!

NARRATOR (*struggling*): No . . . please . . .

GOMER: First you've got to promise me you'll never get married!

NARRATOR: Why?

GOMER: You should always stay as young and beautiful as you are this morning!

NARRATOR (*embarrassed*): I'm not beautiful . . .

GOMER: Of course you are! Why do you think I love you so much? It's because you're beautiful and honey-tongued, and you quote me poetry when my master has gone to town. I tingle all over . . . and feel young again!

NARRATOR: All I . . .

GOMER: Don't ever get married . . . promise? For me?

NARRATOR: I already said I wouldn't.

GOMER: Good! Now quote me something.

NARRATOR: Here?

GOMER: There's nothing to worry about. Come on.

NARRATOR: Well . . . what do you want to hear?

GOMER (*flirting*):   Silly boy . . . why should it matter? Quote me whatever you want . . . whatever you feel. (*They have their arms around each other.*)

NARRATOR (*clearing throat*):   Oh, my dove, that art in the clefts of the rock (HOSEA *enters upstage left, unseen*), in the secret places of the stairs, let me see thy countenance, let me hear thy voice; for sweet is thy voice, and thy countenance is comely.

GOMER (*smiling*):   Mmmm. Keep going.

NARRATOR: Take us the foxes, the little foxes that spoil the vines, for our vines have tender grapes.

GOMER: My beloved is mine and I am his. (*Taking his hand.*) Come, my love, and swiftly, for the master is gone and won't return till sundown.

(*They exit upstage right; HOSEA watches them go and moves up right.*)

HOSEA (*quietly—holding his emotion*):   Then he was right. He was right. (*Breaking, shouting as he falls to his knees.*) Oh, God! (*Sobbing.*) Why do you have to be right? (*He slumps on floor, head in hands, sobbing.*)

(NARRATOR *enters upstage right to upstage center above him; once again, he is God.*)

NARRATOR: Then you've seen.

HOSEA (*stops sobbing, pauses*): I've seen.

NARRATOR: And now?

HOSEA (*through his teeth*): I'll kill her.

NARRATOR: No, Hosea.

HOSEA (*paying no attention*): I'll strip her naked and throw her into the center of the marketplace!

NARRATOR: You will keep her as your wife.

HOSEA: No one shall deliver her out of my hand!

NARRATOR: She will bear you a daughter . . .

HOSEA: I'll have no pity on her!

NARRATOR: . . . and yet another son . . .

HOSEA: I'll not claim him!

NARRATOR: And you will love her still.

HOSEA: Where once I loved, now I hate!

NARRATOR: Many waters cannot quench love; neither can floods of tears drown it. Love is as strong as death.

HOSEA (*crumbling to his knees*): I love her! Why? Why? (*Sobbing.*)

NARRATOR (*moving downstage right, looking away*): You

will call the girl's name Lo-Ruhamah—not pitied. And the boy's name will be Lo-Ammi—not my people. For I will have no more mercy upon the house of Israel, but I will utterly take them away—for they are not my people, and I will not be their God!

HOSEA (*still sobbing*): Why has she done this thing?

NARRATOR: I will have no mercy upon Israel's children. Their mother has played the harlot.

HOSEA: Haven't I given to her all she needed or desired?

NARRATOR: I will hedge up Israel's way with thorns. She will follow after her lovers, but will not be able to reach them. Then she will say, "I will return to my first husband, for then it was better for me than now!"

HOSEA: Could I take her back now? After this? No. No, never!

NARRATOR: Doesn't Israel know that *I* gave her the corn and wine and oil? That it was I who multiplied her silver and her gold, which she prepared for Baal? I will no longer give her rich harvests of grain in its season or wine at the harvest of grapes! I will expose her nakedness in public for all her lovers to see! No one will be able to rescue her out of my hand! No one!

HOSEA (*on his knees, finally looking at* NARRATOR: *speaking intensely*): No one. (*He pauses and watches* NARRATOR, *who stares off into space. Then he speaks quietly, but his voice gradually grows louder*): The day of the Lord is coming. Israel shall bring forth her children to the murderer! God shall cast them away because they didn't return to him! He will destroy them, and they shall be wanderers among the nations!

NARRATOR: Do you understand my fury, Hosea? Do you see now my reason for destroying Israel?

HOSEA (*shaken with emotion, nodding*): Destroy Israel, Lord! Destroy her completely!

NARRATOR (*pausing*): No. I will court Israel again and bring her back to me.

HOSEA: No! Surely not now!

NARRATOR: I will give her back her vineyards, and she will sing to me as she did in the days of her youth after I freed her from the captivity in Egypt.

HOSEA: But I don't understand . . .

NARRATOR: In that day she will call me "my husband." She will forget her idols, and their names will never be spoken again. O, Israel! I will bind you to me forever with bonds of righteousness and justice and mercy—and love. You will know me then as you never have before. I will have mercy on those that deserve no mercy; and to them who were not my people I will say, "You are my people!"

HOSEA: Then you can still forgive? After all of this?

NARRATOR: I can, Hosea. I will. And you will, too.

HOSEA: Forgive her? Never. Never! (*He charges off upstage left.*)

NARRATOR (*to himself*): Yes, you will, Hosea. Yes, you will. (*He begins to march across the stage, left to right, right to left, pantomiming a spear on his shoulder, in character of soldier.*)

(*GOMER enters downstage right, below the platform, moves quietly to the edge of stage, and whispers loudly.*)

GOMER: Psst. Captain! (NARRATOR *whirls around, points his spear at audience.*)

NARRATOR: Who goes there!

GOMER: Just a woman, Captain—just one lonely old woman.

NARRATOR: Step up here closer, so I can see your face. (GOMER *moves upstage right to climb downstage right stairs of platform, close to* NARRATOR.) What are you doing? Don't you know the city is under siege by the Assyrians?

GOMER: Yes, Captain . . .

NARRATOR: What are you doing here, anyway? Speak up!

GOMER: I'm looking for a friend of mine . . .

NARRATOR (*sarcastically*): On the city walls?

GOMER: I was told he joined the guards.

NARRATOR: Not a chance. No one's joined the guards for at least a year . . . (*Bitterly.*) People are smarter than that. I mean, who wants to get killed?

GOMER: He may have joined that long ago. I haven't seen him in three years . . . that's when my husband let him go. I looked for him, but never could find out where he'd gone.

NARRATOR: How come your husband fired him?

GOMER (*evasively*): He was our houseboy. Anyway, I finally . . .

NARRATOR: You didn't answer my question . . . say, you and

this houseboy fella. You had something going with him, didn't you?

GOMER: Of course not!

NARRATOR: Sure, I see it now. That's why you're trying to find him. And you're so afraid your husband will find out, you won't even go to his barracks! Sneaking around . . . Hey! Come here; let me get a closer look at you . . .

GOMER (*starting to exit quickly downstage right*): I'd better go!

NARRATOR: Stop!

GOMER: No time to . . .

NARRATOR: Halt or I'll put this spear right between your shoulder blades. (*She stops—he comes to her, turns her around, and peers into her face.*) Yeah, I know you. What's your name? Speak up! What's your name?

GOMER: Terese!

NARRATOR (*shaking head*): That isn't it! What is it, huh? Tell me!

GOMER: It's . . . Gomer.

NARRATOR: Gomer . . . yeah, that's it. Gomer. You're a harlot.

GOMER (*quietly*): Used to be.

NARRATOR: Used to be! You still are, to my way of thinking. That's why you wouldn't come around the barracks—because I told you if I ever caught you again I'd throw you on the block.

GOMER: No! That wasn't me . . .

NARRATOR: Well, you know where you're going now?

GOMER: No!

NARRATOR: That's right, on the slave block. Let's go.

GOMER: No! (*She struggles as he pulls her downstage right.*)
If my husband finds out about this, he'll . . .

NARRATOR: If your husband comes after you again he's
crazy! No one makes the same mistake twice. (*They exit.*)

GOMER: No! (HOSEA *enters upstage left and crosses down to*
audience.)

HOSEA: Sound the alarm! They are coming! Like a vulture,
the enemy descends upon the people of God because they
have broken his covenant and trespassed against his laws!
Now Israel pleads, saying, "Lord, help us, for you are our
God!" But it is too late! Israel has thrown off the good and
run after evil—now evil shall run after her! She has sown
the wind, and now she reaps the whirlwind for her sins!
(NARRATOR *enters upstage right, running.* HOSEA
blocks his path.) Where are you going?

NARRATOR: To the wall, you fool, to defend the city!

HOSEA: No use! It's too late!

NARRATOR: Have they taken the wall already?

HOSEA: Not yet, but soon! Israel is destroyed; Samaria is destroyed! Too late for her! Too late!

NARRATOR: You're crazy! Let me go! If they haven't taken
the wall yet, there's still a chance! (*Breaks past* HOSEA,
who grabs his hand.)

HOSEA: No chance!

NARRATOR (*backhanding* HOSEA, *who falls to his knees*):
Fool! (*Exits.*)

HOSEA (*after him, on his knees*): You're the fool! You are
doomed! You will disappear like morning mist, like dew
that quickly dries away! Like chaff, blown by the wind! Like
a cloud of smoke!

NARRATOR (*offstage*): O, Lord! Save us!

HOSEA (*enjoying the sight*): Now you turn to him! Now you
call on him! But it is too late. You're doomed! You who
mocked the prophets and scorned his messengers are
doomed!

NARRATOR (*offstage*): Over there! Over there! Strengthen
the left flank; they're coming up! O, God, hurry!

HOSEA (*quieter*): Why do you continue to call upon God now?
O, Israel, you adulterous woman! You scorn your husband
until times of trouble, but then you scream, "My husband
will help me! My husband will save me!" You're wrong! You
have been sentenced to slavery by the Lord! Your own
husband sends you into exile! Who'll save you now?

NARRATOR (*offstage*): They're turning back! Look to the
right side there; drive them back!

HOSEA (*shocked*): No! No, that isn't possible!

NARRATOR: We're saved! Thank God, we're saved!

HOSEA (*to himself*): No. There must be some mistake! God?
God? God!

NARRATOR (*entering upstage left; he is God now*): I am here,
Hosea.

HOSEA (*angrily*):   Why have you saved them?

NARRATOR: They're my people. They cried out for my help.

HOSEA: Which you *said* you would deny!

NARRATOR: I promised them help! They called upon their Lord . . . and I saved them.

HOSEA: But what about me! You've made a fool out of me! I suppose you know that!

NARRATOR: Is that so terrible? Should I sacrifice a whole city for your pride?

HOSEA: No, I don't mean . . . you *said* you were going to!

NARRATOR: Is this the same Hosea who pleaded for the life of the city he loved? This man who cries now for its destruction to soothe his wounded ego?

HOSEA (*pausing*):   All right. All right. If that's the way it is, that's fine. Only don't go calling on *me* anymore, God! I'm sick of you always calling on *me,* anyway!

NARRATOR: Is it so bad, Hosea?

HOSEA: Bad? You made me marry a prostitute! And then you ruined the marriage! You drove me insane with concern for my beloved country; then you made me hate it! And now, after I've worked for you, preached for you, been mocked because of you, you turn your back on me and make me the laughingstock of the city! You don't think that's bad?

NARRATOR: And of the things I've given you in return— what of them?

HOSEA: What have you given me?

NARRATOR: Two sons, a daughter . . .

HOSEA: One son! That's right, one! The only thing I have left in the world to love!

NARRATOR: And what of him . . . of that son? What if I were to require him of you, as I required Isaac from Abraham?

HOSEA (*pausing*): Oh—no. No. You wouldn't do that. You couldn't do that!

NARRATOR: And if I did?

HOSEA: Then . . . then put sackcloth on my body! Let me grovel in the ash heap! Cover my body with sores and call me Job, for I've suffered far more!

NARRATOR: Job suffered in patience and without cause!

HOSEA: Without cause? Then I've suffered *with* cause? Oh, God, what *cause?*

NARRATOR: To show mankind how much I've suffered . . . how much your God has suffered. Oh, but not yet. Yes, Hosea, you've suffered a lot for my sake. But who has suffered more than God? I made the world and gave it as a gift to men . . . yet my people scorn my name. I made you and your race to have fellowship with me, Hosea. And still men turn their backs! I chose Israel out of all the nations and set her aside to be my own. I cherished her and loved her as a husband loves his wife . . . and she too turned from me.

HOSEA: Then punish her! Destroy her!

NARRATOR: But I still love her, Hosea. And not just Israel. I love the whole world. My people have enslaved themselves to sin and death—and still I love them. I will buy them back, Hosea. Oh, not with a few pieces of silver and a measure of barley—that would never pay the price. I will buy my people back with the blood of my own son.

HOSEA: We're not worth it.

NARRATOR: You are to me. I will buy back my adulterous wife—just as you will buy back yours.

HOSEA: Not me. Whatever she's gotten herself into is her business, not mine.

NARRATOR: And if she calls to you for help, you'll pass her by?

HOSEA: I will.

NARRATOR: No, Hosea. She's bound to you forever with bonds of love. I forged those chains myself—not even God will break them.

(*He exits upstage right and reenters leading* GOMER, *who pantomimes being bound in chains.* NARRATOR *pushes her to block upstage center, then pushes her up on it.* HOSEA *sees none of this before he begins his lines.*)

HOSEA: With bonds of love. No, I cannot. I will not! After what she's done to me?

NARRATOR: Auction here! Auction here! Fine woman slave for sale! Good teeth, good looks, good strong back! Work in the kitchen or the fields, wherever you put her. What am I offered for this fine piece of merchandise? Do I hear a shekel? A shekel? Anyone pay a shekel?

HOSEA (*turning to look*): Gomer!

GOMER: Hosea!

NARRATOR: I have a shekel; do I hear two? Two shekels for this fine slave. Do I hear two shekels? Two shekels?

GOMER: Hosea . . . help me! (HOSEA *looks at her, slowly turns his back on her, starts to walk offstage left.*)

NARRATOR: I have two shekels; somebody give me three, give me three—three. Do I have four?

GOMER: Hosea! (*He stops.*)

NARRATOR: I have four. Somebody make it five. Anybody for five? Strong back, good worker! Do I hear five?

GOMER: Hosea, please!

NARRATOR: I have five! Do I hear a six? Anyone for six? (HOSEA *turns to look at her.*) Somebody give me a six. A six? (GOMER *mouths "Please!"*) Going once . . .

HOSEA (*resolutely*): Six.

NARRATOR: I have six! Do I have seven? Seven! Do I hear eight? Can I get an eight?

HOSEA: Eight!

NARRATOR: I have eight; do I hear nine? Nine!

HOSEA: Ten!

NARRATOR: Ten! Do I hear . . . eleven? Do I hear . . .

HOSEA: Twelve!

NARRATOR: Twelve! Do I have thirteen? Thirteen? (HOSEA *pantomimes checking his money bag, sighs.*) Thirteen! Do I hear fourteen? Fourteen? Going once at thirteen. Going twice . . .

HOSEA: I'll give you fifteen shekels.

NARRATOR: Fifteen! I have fifteen shekels! Anybody bid against this man with fifteen shekels? Do I hear sixteen? Going once at fifteen, going twice . . . sold to the man for fifteen shekels. (GOMER *jumps off the block and runs to* HOSEA, *who embraces her. She is sobbing as* NARRATOR *comes down to* HOSEA.) Your money, sir? (HOSEA *pantomimes handing him a bag; he unlocks* GOMER*'s bonds. She leans against* HOSEA, *sobbing. When she is free, he puts his arm around her.*)

HOSEA (*quietly*): I imagine Jezreel will be wondering where we are. Come on, Gomer. Let's go home. (*He supports her strongly as they cross downstage right stairs and up the church aisle, out the back door.*)

NARRATOR (*to audience as the two exit*): It's a beautiful story. But it's not really about Hosea. It's about God. For God so loved the world that he gave Jesus, his own son, to die—to buy the world back from sin and death. Each day we stand on an auction block, selling ourselves more deeply into sin, when the price for our freedom has already been paid! We have a choice. We can remain in slavery . . . or we can claim our freedom in Christ. Your God is calling you to come back to him. Which will you choose to do? (*Blackout or move into an invitation time.*)